Broken Arrow
Press

Praise for D. László Conhaim's
Comanche Captive

"Fast-paced ... unusual ... With *Comanche Captive*, D. László Conhaim makes the unusual choice of telling the story of a woman's resolute quest after she is taken from the band of Indians who had captured her. With drama, humor, and vivid detail, he creates an unflinching view of the harsh complexities of life on the frontier."

— Lucia St. Clair Robson,
bestselling author of *Ride the Wind*

"A deftly crafted and simply riveting read from cover to cover ... very highly recommended."

— *Midwest Book Review*

"Conhaim offsets this brutal tale of human cruelty, injustice, and violence with rich descriptions of the natural beauty of the West. Recommended."

— *Library Journal*

"*Comanche Captive*'s rich characterizations bring a fascinating period of American history to life ... page turning ... thought provoking."

— Michael Belfiore,
author of *The Department of Mad Scientists*

"A resolute woman teams up with a retired soldier in this Western set in post–Civil War Texas ... Conhaim is a cinematic writer, and his descriptions are captivating ... [he] displays substantial knowledge of the tribes he writes about and creates Native American characters who are as fully developed as his white players. An engrossing tale of the Old West."

— *Kirkus Reviews*

Praise for
All Man's Land

Selected Finalist Best Traditional
Western Novel, 2020 Western
Writers of America Spur Awards

"Maverick" Finalist Will Rogers Medallion Awards

"Conhaim draws on various elements of the classic Western
... to tell a story inspired by his longtime fascination with
the singer and activist Paul Robeson ... Benjamin is a
compelling, multilayered protagonist who moves beyond his
Robeson inspiration ... The prose is vivid and often dramatic,
which makes for a memorable read ... A well-developed and
thoughtful novel of right and wrong in the Old West."
—*Kirkus Reviews*

"Inspired by the music and life of Paul Robeson, D. László
Conhaim's *All Man's Land* ... reminds the reader that the most
unlikely of relationships can form even in spaces where they
should not exist ... Seeing the humanity in another person
is a meaningful sub-theme ... We are battling, still, with
many of the themes addressed in this book ... I thoroughly
enjoyed [it] ... It is a book that should be read in classrooms
and community book clubs. It is one to add to the discussion
of race relations as this country should be *All Man's Land*."
—Christian Starr,
ThyBlackMan.com

"A fictional tribute to renaissance man Paul Robeson, *All Man's Land* is a solid literary work ... of social inspection, historical precedent, and cultural insights ... As Benjamin Neill wields the Jewish Kaddish and guns alike, readers will delight in a story that is far more literary and intellectual than the typical Western entertainment. *All Man's Land* weaves a powerful story of how times change, and how one man's purpose becomes an inspiring message for new generations."

—*Midwest Book Review*

"The exploration of a black-Jewish relationship in frontier times would seem challenge enough, but Conhaim blends this reality-based novel with a striking consideration of the overall prejudices and sentiments of the times, injecting fictional drama and embellishments into a kind of memoir that is absorbing and enlightening on many levels ... As Conhaim paints a portrait of David, a young man who prompts Benjamin Neill to examine his own prejudices and purposes, readers receive a solid blend of frontier conflict and the evolution of challenging relationships ... *All Man's Land* returns to a world that has largely moved away from Western popular fiction and memories of Paul Robeson, but it lives on as a tribute to this powerful individual and resurrects a sense of his multifaceted talents while providing a social commentary on America's early years."

—*Donovan's Bookshelf*

"D. László Conhaim pens a sequel to *Comanche Captive* in the form of a tribute novella to Paul Robeson: *All Man's Land*. Robeson, an African-American bass baritone concert artist and actor, was recognized for his musical performances and cultural accomplishments, but his political activism made him a controversial figure admired by some and reviled by others. Set in turn-of-the-century Wyoming, *All Man's Land* personifies Robeson in the character Benjamin Neill—Civil War hero, a learned man, a masterful singer, a political progressive, a man of the people and a prophet—who comes to town to settle a score. Conhaim packs gunfights, villains, intrigue, mystery, plot twists, some romance and a happy ending into this vivid, entertaining read."

—Michael Searles, *Roundup Magazine*,
Western Writers of America

"Conhaim transfers [Paul Robeson's] story to the American West and incarnates Robeson in the fictitious Benjamin Neill, son of a slave, and a war veteran whose talent and courage parallel Robeson's. Conhaim's prose is spare but potent and the pages turn in the blink of an eye. I couldn't help but be reminded of the great TV show "Deadwood" for the authenticity of his supporting players, but at its heart it is a story about freedom and values."

—Terrance Gelenter, *The Paris Insider Readers Circle*

COMANCHE
CAPTIVE

A novel

D. László Conhaim

COMANCHE CAPTIVE

Paperback Edition
Copyright © 2020 by D. László Conhaim
All rights reserved

Broken Arrow Press, 2566 West Lake of the Isles
Pkwy, Minneapolis, MN 55405, USA

brokenarrow908@gmail.com

Cover and interior design by Velin@Perseus-Design.com
Logo by Michael R. Geffen
Author photo by Bridget M. Mayer
Cover photo (Palo Duro Canyon) © Terry Thompson
www.TerryThompsonPhoto.com
Cover design contributor: Nicole Nodland
www.nicolenodland.com

First paperback edition published June 2020

ISBN 978-0-9843175-2-3

While inspired by historical events and people, *Comanche Captive* is a work of fiction whose characters, their histories, and the opinions they express are attributable solely to the author's imagination

Visit the author's website: dlaszloconhaim.com

For my son, Ziv

Note

For principal source material, *Comanche Captive* draws from accounts of the U.S. Army's Red River campaign of 1874 and a host of true stories of Indian captives, both "rescued" and never found. Though the author has striven for accuracy, historical and otherwise, embellishments are numerous. Originally published in hardback by Cengage/Five Star in 2017, this is the first installment of a trilogy featuring the so-called buffalo soldiers of the U.S. Cavalry. In 2019, the author's own imprint, Broken Arrow Press, released *All Man's Land*, chronologically the third in the series. In late 2021, a direct sequel to *Comanche Captive* is slated for publication to complete the trilogy. Each title examines conflicts between races and cultures, *intra*cultural strife, and resultant questions of identity, loyalty, and belonging.

The two oceans are already linked together by an Iron Highway. The savage, alarmed at this new encroachment, is ready at any moment for a desperate, probably a final effort to drive out the invaders of his hunting grounds. Fearful of his future he opposes such encroachments for in them he sees no benefit to the remnant of his race, who have taken refuge on the plains and in the mountains ... Their savage natures, incapable of restraint, render them by instinct foes to progress and the cause of humanity ... As with the buffalo the approach of civilization is to them the knell of destruction.

— De B. Randolph Keim,
"Sheridan's Views on the Indian Question,"
Washington Evening Star, May 9, 1870

... the reservation system is the only one offering any prospects of success, but all experience has shown that the wild Indian will not adopt it until he is forced to do so. All the tribes on the Northern Pacific coast had to be subdued and forced on the reservations, which was accomplished between the years 1855–1860, then peace ensued. Latterly the same policy has been pursued in regard to the Comanches, Kiowas, Cheyennes, and Arrapahoes. After the wild Indians are put upon the reservations a strong military force will have to be kept there to protect the agents and others required in the work of civilization, and also for the subordination of the Indians, and their protection against the encroachments of the white settlers, who otherwise would take possession of their lands.

— Lt. General Phil H. Sheridan, 1870

Prologue

Known for its "moral" treatments, the three-story Kirkby Sanitarium for the Curable and Incurable Insane sat on spacious grounds across the Trinity River from Fort Worth. Recently built and half vacant, its presence on the frontier seemed to anticipate the costs in human hardship that western expansion would exact from the white man—and the white woman. Already, one of its high-ceilinged quarters held a famous patient. Standing before her only window, Laura Little studied the tranquil cityscape through iron grating. She was wearing riding pants.

Beyond the hospital's back lawn, fringed by cedar, elm, and white mulberry, was the bend of the river, and between the opposite bank and Belknap Street a herd of cattle grazed in morning mist. North lay the airy city grid, ending at the tracks of the Texas and Pacific Railroad, on which a locomotive was puffing toward the sunrise. Prominent among the building clusters was the Trans-continental Hotel, a symbol of the boom expected from improved rail and stage communications with California, Arizona, and the east. According to the weekly notice in the *Democrat*, the Fort Worth–Santa Fe stagecoach made a stop there at ten A.M.

Minutes before nine, a knock at the door preceded the sound of a key turning in its lock. The door clicked open, and with a keyring's jangle a matronly nurse appeared from behind it. Her eyes widened. "Wearing pants again? The director will be disappointed. But, as we say, comfort is our business."

"My boot," said Laura, indicating her loosely clad foot. "Did you bring that lacing?"

"What was I saying about your comfort?" the nurse responded, digging in the pocket of her apron. She motioned toward the hospital bed, noticing the sheets tossed upon it. "Sleeping on the floor again? That can't be comfortable."

Laura sat at the edge of the mattress, extending her boot, open at the tongue.

Crouching, the nurse remarked, "This one won't quite reach the top. We prohibit long laces and stockings, you know. I really should ask you for the other one." She tapped the patient's other boot.

"If I haven't hanged myself yet, I'm not likely to."

"Don't forget why you were admitted here in the first place."

"That was months ago," replied Laura. "Silly me."

The nurse tightened the lace and beamed up at her. "Progress is being made, then?"

"I understand Dr. Kirkby wants to see me this morning because I'm not—making progress, that is."

The nurse tied the knot. "The governor insisted. Our director sees very few patients himself." She rose and took Laura's hands, pulling her upright from the bed. "Time to smile! It's the start of a lovely day. Shall we pin your hair for the interview?"

Laura shook her head of wild, blond curls.

"Very well, then." The nurse's dissatisfaction was evident in her tone. "Following your session with Dr. Kirkby, you may enjoy a spell in the courtyard. It's reserved for women till three. They've got the fountain running again, and there's a new bed of pink lilies—from the Orient, they say. And this afternoon, following rest time, we have a piano recital in the lounge. Mozart." She pronounced the name *moh-zart*.

"How nice," said Laura. "I'll get to see all my fellow lunatics."

"Don't say that!" the nurse replied, leading her to the door. "If you aren't a lunatic—"

"If?"

Hands on hips, the nurse said, "That's not what I meant, miss. You simply need a bit more reconditioning. Who wouldn't after what you've been through?"

"Are you a doctor?"

"Of course not. I just—"

"Then I will thank you to leave doctoring to the doctors. May we go now?"

The nurse pursed her lips and shut the door behind them.

The Curable Women's Ward was cheerfully bright thanks to big windows at both landings, where the corridors terminated. At this hour of the day quiet prevailed on the premises, except for the occasional scream from the Incurable Ward. Following breakfast, curable patients were returned to their rooms or admitted to the library or garden. To reach the director's office, the nurse and Laura crossed the courtyard toward the south-facing administrative building in the four-part complex. As they passed the central fountain, the nurse acknowledged the stone representation of a family of four, all reaching for the sky, arcs of water spouting from their open palms. "You see! And yonder are those flowers I mentioned!" But Laura's attention was occupied by shadowy figures watching her from the windows of the Curable Men's Ward, opposite. Posted at each entrance was a male attendant.

At the domed secretariat a pockmarked young man held the door open for them, the chattering nurse leading. Laura noticed the guard's reflection in the angled glass panes. He was lewdly looking her up and down from behind.

She turned toward him. "Want to keep those eyes?"

He reacted with a guilty smile, bobbing on his heels. "You sure don't look like no squaw in them pants ..."

With a devious twitch of her lips she jerked both her fists, one forward, the other back, as if tautening a bowstring. The orderly shied a step. Then, to his startled look, she flashed the fingers of her right hand as if releasing an arrow point blank at him.

"Pow," she said. Then she pivoted and entered the lobby behind the oblivious nurse.

Gloominess prevailed here despite diffused natural light afforded by stained-glass windows on either side of the double doors, which were locked day and night. Crowned by an unlit chandelier, the vaulted chamber received additional illumination from scattered oil lamps, which did little to brighten the place and instead made it feel rather like a funeral parlor. A couch and armchairs were arranged around a dormant fireplace to the left, and framed pictures of the brick and stone edifice's construction were proudly hung on the walls.

"This way," instructed the nurse.

To the right was the reception desk, behind it the staff entrance guarded by a more imposing orderly. They approached the receptionist, a smiling young woman who blushed as they drew near. "Nine A.M. appointment with Dr. Kirkby ..." the nurse announced.

The young woman rose to her feet, hands clasped at her waist. "Why, it's Miss Little!" She stammered as she went on. "I've been so curious to meet you, I mean, having read so much about you in the Democrat. You are as beautiful as they say."

"It's nine o'clock," Laura reminded her.

"Oh, it is indeed!" She waved them around the desk. Laura could feel the girl's starstruck eyes following her. As she and the nurse vanished from view, she overheard the receptionist tell the guard to post himself outside Dr. Kirkby's door.

The interior corridor was plush, with red carpet and brass fixtures. A few staff members, taken aback by the presence in this building of the notorious patient, paused long enough to realize they were staring before hastily ducking into offices on either side. Canvas and tintype portraits lined the walls between door frames, acknowledging the founders and legendary practitioners of the so-called moral methods employed here, among them Frenchmen Jean Baptiste Pussin, Philippe Pinel, and Jean Esquirol; Englishmen William and Samuel Tuke; and Americans William Rush and Dorothea Dix.

With the lumbering attendant following, Laura and the nurse continued to the end of the hallway. They paused at the director's door and exchanged looks before the nurse knocked. A muted voice from within called to admit the patient. After a crosswise glance at the guard, Laura slid past the nurse and closed the door herself.

Awash in sunlight, Dr. Kirkby's corner office overlooked the southwestern grounds, including a thatched stable situated where the driveway looped back near the riverside trees. The bank of windows, plank floor, and low ceiling all gave it the look of a captain's cabin at the stern of an old frigate. An enormous oak desk, centered snugly before the windows, added to the effect.

"You're looking well, young lady!" crowed the silhouetted figure of Dr. Kirkby as he rose, tall and sturdy. "And wearing saddle pants! Planning on taking a horse out, perhaps?"

"Sure am," she replied, stepping forward purposefully. The scarf she wore around her neck was as blue as her drawstring blouse.

He chuckled. Rounding the desk with grace, he gave her the sympathetic smile of a priest. "I myself delight in the ride to work every day. A prescription of saddle time might just restore the balance of your senses."

"I'm sure it would," she said. "The nurses don't allow me much sunlight."

Now an arm's reach away, Dr. Kirkby shook his finger in the air. "Prolonged exposure to the sun has a withering effect upon the brain. In fact, our records indicate you were admitted with a severe case of what we call parched-brain syndrome, the effects of which include disaffection and delusion. That said, we keep our dormitories flooded with light and our grounds well tended because natural light and the natural beauty of the earth promote recovery."

He paused to fill his lungs, the intake straining his vest buttons. Broad, ruddy, and uncommonly clean shaven, he occupied every inch of his long-tailed coat, the kind of frame you'd have to climb to go over. Up close, an ugly bruise under one eye caught the light. Instinctively she drew back.

"The governor's office is in touch with us weekly," he offered in a sanguine tone, then added, "and you'll be pleased to know your family plans a visit Saturday."

"When they arrive," she said, "tell them I'm gone."

Dr. Kirkby straightened to his full height. "As you are aware, Miss Little, I'm taking a personal interest in your rehabilitation."

"Another examination?"

"Heavens, no." He reached for a tin of chocolates on his desk and opened it to her.

She declined.

He forced a smile, motioned toward the pair of stuffed armchairs facing the desk, and sat with one leg draping its corner. Laura tentatively accepted a seat below him. Their chin-to-chin distance was about the same as before. Annoying at best. Challenging if he rose suddenly.

She detected a light breeze from a window behind him, open a crack.

"I'd offer you a cup of tea," said Dr. Kirkby with an unattractive chortle, "but, frankly, a patient struck me with hers last week." He traced the curve of his orbital bone as if taking some pleasure in the sensation. She noted a wedding band on one finger.

"Now I understand the security measures," she responded, "and the shiner too."

It didn't take much to make him blush. "Everyone should feel comfortable here, including those of us who put our own safety on the line."

This was her chance. "I have something here that calms my nerves even better than tea," she said.

Dr. Kirkby ticked his chin to one side and furrowed his brow. "You do?"

She nodded, her eyes a penetrating green in the bright morning light. "It's a silly little thing, really ..." She patted a bulge in her hip pocket.

His gaze followed her fingers as she pushed them inside. He shifted, apparently restless, and glanced toward the door. If he was about to call the guard, it was too late. From her pocket she produced a balled pair of socks. Her plump lips parted as she smiled and held them up. "It soothes me to squeeze it," she said.

He leaned back, mildly relieved yet still suspicious. "Does it?"

"Oh, yes." She watched him as he eyed the pulsing veins behind her knuckles. "In your book," she said, "would my use of this object be considered beneficial?"

He swallowed and replied, "In my book, whether you wear your hair down or up matters more."

"I was told I could be myself here."

Again he chuckled. "I doubt your physician put it quite like that. Allow me to explain. When you choose to wear your hair up again—not as a mere ruse, mind you, but because you are truly determined to rejoin society—you will have exhibited a promising gain. We do not wish your stay here to be protracted."

"In other words, the governor of Texas wishes it to end shortly."

He answered as a professional, chin raised. "To discharge you, I must be confident your improvement is genuine, that you are a threat neither to yourself nor to the public. It's so for every patient."

"Wearing pants hurts no one," she said. "Neither does wearing one's hair down."

"Neither does sleeping on the floor," he replied. "I've heard about that as well. But following the incident that brought you to us, we should like to see behavioral adjustments in the right direction. To sustain the balance of your senses outside these walls, you must feel at ease with the expectations of polite society." He flicked imaginary lint from his knee, where one leg crossed the other. "You might even try on a dress for a change. You'd look lovely in one, I expect."

If he'd hoped to flatter her, he was mistaken. "After living with the Indians," she retorted, "you don't go back to wearing prim and proper dresses."

"Not you," he countered. Then, with sincerity, "How about a skirt for starters? Indians wear skirts ..."

She sat straighter in her chair. "Only if I get to braid my hair at the sides and put on a Thanksgiving show for all the other inmates."

Frowning, he shook his head. "Your file calls you clever. Witty too. You certainly are." He clasped his hands. "Miss Little, are you at least coming to terms with why you are here?"

"I have the scar to prove it. Every tingle is a reminder."

"I am not referring to the suicide attempt. That's merely what brought you to us. The underlying question is, what led you to it?"

"I lost hope. But I've got it back now. I have a vision."

He grimaced despite himself. "Having hope is crucial. Hope in the practical, the attainable. Not in the impossible. Your despair begins with your failure to recognize there is no other way."

Glancing at the wall clock, she asked, "Isn't there?"

He replied with a trace of aggressiveness. "Fort Worth is the edge of civilization. Beyond us live savages whose way of life is ending." He raised a hand to stave off her protest. "*Ending*, Miss Little. Rapidly. In short, there's no future in it. Not for them, and not for you."

"There are treaties, reservations ..."

"That is a different way of life. Nobody—certainly not I— will consider you mentally competent so long as you intend to live with them again, anywhere. Hence, I ask you, just what is the other way?"

Clenching her fists, she replied, "I know you mean well, Doctor. But what difference is there, to me, between your perspective and that of the man on the street? What am I doing here if it isn't different? How am I ever to get out if it doesn't change? Like everyone else, you're convinced I should 'take it like it is.' Well, I have a son out there. And I'm going back to him." She paused for a breath. "Do you know how?"

He spoke right into her trap. "Ho—"

She sprang like a panther onto his chest and shoved the socks between his teeth. Then she jacked her arms and thrust him back against the desk, sending his billfold flying.

Only once before had she committed a violent act, and this one felt right too.

Dr. Kirkby thrust his hands between her forearms and tried to force her jaw back. Before he could gain the advantage, she clawed his lapels and used her weight to send them both over the edge of the desk.

Their entwined bodies rolled into free fall, and her victim thudded shoulder first onto the planking. The brutal impact of her body crashing on his chest made him groan like a wild boar, or so it sounded to her. She planted her feet at his sides and grasped his left shoulder with both hands. Winded as he was, nostrils flaring, his squirming resistance failed to counter her strenuous effort to turn him on his belly; but now, prone on the floor and beginning to revive, he planted his meaty hands parallel to his shoulders and pushed himself upward. He was partway to his knees when she splayed him again with a heel to the tailbone. This gave her a moment to pull a double-noosed lace from her other pocket. Contrary to what she'd told the nurse, it hadn't broken at all.

She herself had once been struck and bound, and she'd witnessed others struck and bound and worse with regularity. Now she threw herself onto Dr. Kirkby's back. When he tried to gain purchase of her, she caught his wrist in the boot-lace noose and yanked the left tail tight through a surgeon's knot. Whimpering, he shifted his weight to the shoulder of his bound arm, trying to catch her with his flailing free hand. She ensnared that one as well and rose triumphantly with a boot planted on his spine. She leaned back against his weight and lashed his wrists together as if binding a boar for roasting.

His ring finger protruded from the jumble of digits. The wedding band could be useful. She spit on his knuckles and ripped it from his knobby finger. Muffled by the floorboards, his scraping, burning cry was heard by her alone. He jackknifed one leg and made another attempt to rise. Grasping both lace tails, she leapt onto the small of his back and flattened him again. Now straddling his torso, she pushed his bound wrists forward till his arms stopped in their sockets. He growled in pain, and attempted to kick her from behind.

She hadn't counted on the danger posed by his long, strong legs, but neither had she planned to use the monumental weight of the desk to her right. With the lace tails held in both fists, she thrust herself sideways into the gap between their bodies and the desk, an action that turned him on his side so he faced the bank of windows behind it. She wedged her heel between his shoulder blades and managed to double-knot the lace around one of the desk's stubby, iron feet.

As she rose, his boot found her gut.

Spinning from the blow, she tripped backward over his writhing body and landed near his side. Directly above her was the open window.

Meantime, Dr. Kirkby, hardly pacified, had righted himself and was tugging against the desk rather than attempting to kick her again. Clutching her abdomen and heaving for air, she got to her feet and retrieved his wallet from the floor. While his glassy-eyed gaze flitted this way and that, she emptied the wallet of its bills and stuffed them in her pocket. With them, she could buy a seat on the stagecoach.

She bounced the empty wallet off his chest and slipped his wedding ring onto her own finger. "Apologies to Mrs. Kirkby," she said.

He redoubled his jerking movements to free himself, straining into a squat with his shoulders flat against the top of the desk. His cheeks flushed and swelled with the effort. Finally he collapsed, sweat coursing over his brow. It was almost amusing to witness.

Satisfied he was her prisoner, she untied the scarf from around her neck, draped it over her tossed, blond hair, and secured it under her chin. A second later she pulled the window toward her on its hinges and lifted herself into its frame.

She cleared the hedge by an inch. Her knees ached from breaking the fall. Catching her breath, she hesitated in the warmth of the sun. Fifty feet away over her left shoulder were the steps up to the building's entrance. Parked below the façade was the temptation of an idle buggy drawn by a sheeny, fly-swatting pair of horses. Even if she could make it past all those office windows unnoticed, detaching a mount would take time; and though she still might get away, the absence of one of the team could raise the alarm far sooner than her appointment with Dr. Kirkby would end. The time she had left on his clock was equal to what she needed to reach the Trans-continental Hotel. The stable was still her best chance. She glanced left and right over the verdant lawns and then proceeded down the dirt path toward the solitary structure. Head pounding from fear and excitement, she was barely conscious of the pretty birdsong from the woods beyond.

At this final door of her escape route, she froze. What if a stablehand was inside? Never mind, she had to risk whatever noise would result from rolling the door. A two-handed tug set it clanging in motion, and she slipped through.

The scent of freshly cut hay made her sneeze, but it was just another sound in a room filled with whinnies and snorts, hoof stamping and chewing, and the odd rattle of a bolt lock. Some of the horses were restless. At the far end of a wood floor between opposing rows of stalls was an open back gate that threw accents of light across the dim space. Above, a hay loft and rafters. Each stall was labeled with the horse owner's name. The first on the right read *Dr. Kirkby.* Over the sign on the transom poked the head of a tall quarter horse with tender, oval eyes.

Laura took a moment to get acquainted. She rubbed her curled fingers against the horse's spongy, warm muzzle, then the palm of her hand against his hard cheek. Finally she held his great head in both hands. He nodded it out of her grasp. She unbolted the gate. The animal advanced toward her, seeking more affection, and she responded by patting his shoulders and caressing his muscular neck. Next, from the dividing wall, she unhooked his bridle and with expert speed fitted the bit and uncoiled the reins.

She was leading him out of the stall when a dark figure blocked the rear exit. "Who's that with ole Brandy?"

The speaker came forward and stopped before her, a mustachioed Negro man with a bald pate, round shoulders, and suspenders lashed to his rotund belly.

She placed her hand across her chest, Dr. Kirkby's wedding band in plain sight. "Why, you sure gave me a scare!" Then she unleashed her luminous smile on him and took a chance. "I'm Mrs. Kirkby."

"That so?" The man tilted his head to one side. "Nice to make your acquaintance, ma'am." Wearing a puzzled look, he continued to scrutinize her.

"My husband didn't tell you I'd be taking Brandy out for his exercise?"

"Why, no, ma'am."

Laura broke contact briefly, spotting a pair of reins hanging in the next stall down. Though she could rely on her agility to avail herself of them, how would she overpower and silence the stablehand? She shouldn't try unless he interfered. A Negro wouldn't, she decided. "Well, you know Dr. Kirkby, his mind always on his work …" It sounded unconvincing even to her. Was it enough for him? She began leading the horse toward the rear gate, passing the stablehand with a feeble smile.

He followed. "But, ma'am, that horse ain't saddled!"

She swung onto the mount with nimble elegance. A few tugs brought the animal under control. "I don't need one," she replied.

Leaving the man scratching his head, she trotted out into the sun and soon vanished into the riverside thicket.

Part I
Miss Little

Chapter One

Alarmed, Scott Renald halted his sorrel and pack mule. A distant plume of smoke billowed against the sunset—too big for a campfire, too concentrated for a grass fire, and two days' ride from the nearest forest. Only the Comancheria way station could kindle such a blaze. He hadn't expected hostiles this early in his journey.

Later, rounding a jagged red-rock outcrop, his horse suddenly whinnied and reversed, sending the mule cling-clanging for footing. Grasping the lead rope in one hand, Renald stood in his stirrups to obtain a better view. Further on, the coach trail was obstructed by a dark, spiny clump. In the failing light, at first he mistook it for an alarmed porcupine, needles raised, or maybe a skunk, but trotting up close he pulled his Winchester.

His horse, ears flattened, whinnied again and reared up. Renald jerked him down. "Easy, Stardust ..."

He glanced warily left and right, then dismounted and knelt beside the deceased. Missing were the man's scalp and sidearm. With a free hand, Renald grasped the stiff, whiskered chin and turned the head with effort. The motion revealed the stricken end-gaze of the Fort Worth–Santa Fe whip whose whole life had come to this. If such was his fate, what of his passengers? Renald let his eyes wander over the tuft of arrows. He reached out and bent one back. The red-tailed hawk fletching, sinew weave, and nock shape identified it as Comanche. When time allowed, a war party could return to the old ways and enjoy a slow kill. The unretrieved arrows made the murder into a statement to all *taiboo nuu*, white men. More, the liberal use of them suggested the hostiles had gained firearms in the raid.

Renald rose and followed the swath of dried blood to where the stage driver had been struck off his horse. In the dirt he could see where the mounted braves, four in all, had assembled abreast for target practice. Here the ground yielded another telling sign. The shodden imprints were those of U.S. Cavalry mounts, doubtless thieved from the station stockade. The braves must've come on foot. From where, was obvious—the nearby reservation at Fort Sill. Unwittingly, Renald had dogged their trail since leaving the post that morning.

He spent the dusk yanking arrows from the body and digging a shallow grave with his telescopic spade. Next, he found a flat place off the path up ahead where he unrolled his mat and opened a can of embalmed beans. Fiery sparks ignited the violet horizon to the west. He would start for the station at sunrise.

* * *

Night passed without event. Renald awoke under a starry sky just before dawn. At the foot of his bedding, his toes in socks jutted out, cold as stones. To the side, scraped and scratched, stood his boots, as if at attention. Rather than rising immediately, he wiggled his digits, worked the muscles of his long legs, and stretched his arms at his sides until the elbows popped. The air smelled of smoke. He pushed aside his woolen blanket and reached for his boots with a groan.

As sunrise gradually revealed his windswept surroundings, he grained and watered his animals, all the while considering what fate had dealt the stationmaster. By first light he was astride Stardust, a big animal, fair of mane and tail, with amber eyes.

If not for the outpost's import on this snaking route to Santa Fe, it would have seemed the most derelict of places, but from miles back, coach travelers and troopers alike anticipated its utility—shade, well water, tins of food, and, for the cavalry, a fresh change of horses. For westbound riders like himself, the post, tucked under a massive overhang in a wide and deep arroyo, was first glimpsed from a sandy, brush-lined cliff forming the eastern wall. Casting his view from it, Renald saw his fears confirmed. The shelter and stockade were reduced to smoking embers. From what he could see, only a singed stagecoach was left standing down there. Angled on collapsed back wheels, it resembled a buffalo carcass stuck in mud flats.

Renald set his jaw and heeled Stardust down the treacherous switchback, letting the mule fall back in line, her load clanking like a chuck wagon. Where the trail leveled out below, he cupped his hand and bellowed the stationmaster's name, futile though it seemed. "Beckert!"

Perhaps the fellow old-timer from C Company had found sanctuary in some nook in the arroyo wall. The echo would discover every one.

Renald rode into the smoldering arena. Bracketing the manmade elements were gaps in the jagged stone wall, natural portals into Comancheria. The corridor to the south led eventually through Blanco Canyon to the Colorado River; the other, northwest onto the tablelands of the Llano Estacado, the Staked Plain. Troopers commonly referred to these trails as South and North Scalp. Each was more likely to bring one in contact with hostiles than the meandering southern commuter approach to Santa Fe, which headed north from here through the pass. Beyond this place only a few white men were accepted by the chiefs. Renald was one of them.

Scattered across the area were open valises, crates, sacks, barrels, and whatnot. Glancing here and there, he zigzagged toward the wreck of the stage, holding high the reins in his gloved hand. Soon he was facing the upturned vehicle, its bare hitch raised, windows shot out, frame splintered by bullet holes. Beyond the through-braces and beams under its belly a butchered body was sprawled in the dirt. Nudging Stardust closer, Renald recognized the dead man as the stage's shotgun rider. As for the fates of the passengers, he'd have to pull the coach off its rear boot to find out.

With a sigh, he jerked the mule close to his side and unclasped the lead from her bridle. He grabbed the lariat coil clipped beside his rifle slip, tied one end to the saddle horn, and fashioned a loop with the other. With a practiced whirl-and-throw he caught the hitch. He reined Stardust around and advanced him. The rope tautened with a groan. Responding to Renald's prods against his ribs, the powerful copper-red beast dragged himself forward a few steps, kicking up dust and ash around his white pasterns. The sounds of creaking wood and straining metal followed. Finally the vehicle came down with a crash, shattering its front wheels. Renald heard the thump of something heavy inside.

He turned his mount back toward the coach and into a cloud of dust stirred by the impact. Once beside the cabin, he tugged the door ajar with a wooden pop. Stardust shied back as a body spilled halfway out. Shards of glass embedded in the man's cheek caught the light. A blackened, crusty patch glistened in place of his scalp. His jaw hung by threads of exposed flesh. Renald peered inside the cabin. Two more victims lay there in a twisted jumble, similarly shot and disfigured. When your killers were Comanche, dying by gunshot alone was lucky. Weeks back, down Casas Rojas way, Renald had come across the remains of two hide men, one buried to his neck as ant food, the other hitched to a buckboard wheel, bird feed.

At least there was no sign of a woman having been aboard— but what of his friend? Maybe he'd dragged himself off to die, somewhere. Renald scanned the space again.

"Beckert!" His call lurched away in both directions.

The wind whistled through the stagecoach.

If Beckert had survived the attack he might've gone to the well. The well ... a sight so familiar it hadn't registered in Renald's first visual sweep. He passed his sandpaper tongue over his lips. How to locate it in this littering of scorched remains? The hole, he recalled, was dug about fifty feet opposite the corral abutting the station house. Though he was packing spyglasses, cavalrymen used the naked eye to identify a threat or an opportunity in a busy landscape. Squinting into the area, he spotted the skeletal remains of the burnt-down fencing and ordered Stardust forward. When they reached the ruins of the pen, he reined the horse back to gain a view from this direction. He immediately discerned the stone cylinder of the well, its pulley rigging still intact and the bucket presumably lowered into the depths, as if dropped in haste—or panic.

He chirruped and went there.

Renald opened the flap of his saddlebag and withdrew his binoculars. From his mounted position beside the well he reviewed his surroundings, patiently for a thirsty man. He saw his mule standing stupidly in the middle distance. He saw the charred stage. He saw the zigzag line of the switchback on the dusty eminence opposite, hard-hit by the sun. Nothing resembled a man's body. The only item that caught his eye, halfway to the mule, was what appeared to be a stuffed burlap sack, the sort used by the U.S. mail service. The very fact it remained unemptied was remarkable. He should leave it where others were sure to find it—in the cabin of the stagecoach. Drawing back from the glasses, he noted its location and determined to pass there when he went for his mule.

He alighted from Stardust and, after an inconclusive look down the well shaft, grabbed the pulley. The shrill squeal of the winch and the effort required to turn it attested to the general neglect that had befallen the outpost under an old-timer's watch. Renald felt his brow bead with sweat as he hoisted the lapping bucket to the edge. He threw off his hat. Holding the pail high with both hands, mouth open, he drenched his sun-browned face and matted, grey hair. The run-off collected in a pool at his feet. His second helping went into the canteens. He pulled a third bucket. Additional containers in need of filling were strapped to the mule yonder. He snatched his hat off the ground and grabbed his saddle gun, letting Stardust drink his share while he went for the pack animal.

Before him was the deep blue of a clear sky, the straw-colored eastern eminence with its switchback trail, and the baked alkaline floor flecked with whatever the fire had sent aloft or the raiders had thrown aside. He crossed this godforsaken gulch cradling his rifle in the crook of his left arm while his right hand swung loose by his short gun. In his path he stepped over or kicked aside flame-licked stage schedules, rusted tools and equipment, army-issue tin dishes, and the like. Fifty paces northward was the ghastly stagecoach, and still ahead his uncomprehending mule, sniffing the warm clay floor for something to eat. Now midway across this wasteland he espied the object of interest, the presumed mail bag, and made for it with quickened steps. As he drew closer, a feeling of alarm arose in him. He paused, wincing in the shade of his hat. This near, blotches of color appeared on the bundle. Blood, he observed—not dried blood, drying blood. Beckert's? Was this all that remained of his friend from C Troop? Or was it something else? A draft animal picked apart by wolves? Renald resumed his approach at an urgent pace, shoulders swinging forward and back, his sense of dread, not relief, rising feverishly as he came up to the suspicious heap.

He stopped just feet away and, despite his exertion, forgot to breathe. His eyes narrowed. A body, for sure. The blackened earth on which the savaged figure lay was a vast bloodstain. He slipped his finger into the trigger ring of his rifle and transferred the weapon to his right side, muzzle up. Then he stepped forward into the muck and looked down. Moments passed before he noticed a gentle rise and fall in the grim cloth. Renald allowed himself some air. He glanced cautiously over his shoulders. Squatting beside the man, his heels rose with difficulty, as if peeling themselves from a spill of paint.

In addition to the other hateful offenses committed against this person, the sign of a gunshot wound below his right shoulder was unmistakable. Untreated, this alone would've been a fatal wound. For the victim it was the first of many abuses. If only he'd had the wherewithal to take his own life rather than run. Attempting escape on foot from the Comanche was worse than a death wish. Renald laid his hand on the back of the human mound and felt life there. The thing shuddered and groaned in response to his touch. He grasped a fistful of sticky cloth and rolled the man over like the stuffed sack he'd mistaken him for. No eyes remained to register the sun. In their places were oozing clots. The man's nose was gone too. He'd been scalped alive.

"Beckert …" moaned Renald. "What've they done to you?"

A line of blood spilled from the old trooper's mouth into his grey whiskers. His lips moved, producing a sound like a voice calling from underwater. He convulsed, gagged. Renald rolled him onto his side. Another bloody expectoration resulted. When Renald restored him to a sky-facing position he was careful to support Beckert's head.

They'd let Beckert keep his tongue. He spoke in a rasp. "Re-*nald*?"

"That's right, Tom. I'm with you." Renald's voice was deep and steady, with a touch of Southern courtliness.

Beckert seemed to smile.

"I'm sure glad I won't pass lonesome," said the stationmaster. "Comanche came for the horses."

"Looks like it."

Beckert coughed, wheezed. "Saw nothing till it was too late."

"That's their way."

"I always dealt good with the Comanche. Now they do me like this."

Renald placed a hand on his chest. "Ones that did it, didn't know you."

"I lived well …" Beckert told himself.

"You go proud, Tom," said Renald. "Anybody taken?"

"Nobody worth taking." His words were filling with fluid. "You been sent out for captives, best turn back."

"Couple German boys gone missing down south," said Renald. "I know the trade routes north. Which Scalp did those bucks follow?"

"North Scalp from the sounds of it." He gagged again. "Too rough for the stage in there ... they loaded up the buckboard. But don't go looking to revenge me, Scott."

"Be sure I will."

Beckert grinned, gruesomely. He drooled more blood and gurgled, "They'll be moving slow."

"I'll catch 'em."

Beckert struggled in a new fit of spasms. "Scott, your sidearm ..."

Renald understood. "Got a rifle too."

"I'm obliged," he gasped.

Renald eased Beckert's head down. He got to his feet, jacking the finger lever, then lowered the barrel and braced the stock against his hip.

"Rest in peace, my friend."

He tore his gaze away, and fired.

There was no time for burial if he was to overhaul the raiders. He turned and pushed through the blistering heat toward his mule, grasping the hot muzzle so hard it hurt.

Chapter Two

Renald followed the war party's trail to the terminus of North Scalp Gorge, which opened onto the desolate plains of Comancheria. Like its narrow entry point near the station, North Scalp ended with a near convergence of its walls. The closer he rode toward the sliver of light the stronger and hotter the draft blew in his face. Given what had happened to Beckert, he thought better of riding out unawares. He strapped the mule's lead rope around his saddle horn and dismounted. Then, motioning Stardust to wait, he eased his head out and stole glances upward right and left before ducking back into cover. He drew a breath and then his gun. This time he stepped fully out, giving the crimson stone walls careful attention. On each side were ledges and crevices from which ambushers could launch an attack. Finding himself alone there, however, he holstered his weapon and beckoned Stardust.

The sun was a fireball in the west. Before him were endless bleached plains dotted by clumps of prickly pear, juniper, and spiny cholla. Twenty minutes' ride north could put him into the so-called Tonk Forest. In its dark sanctuary lived the untamed last of the Tonkawa tribe, the tamed rest permanently sheltered on the Fort Belknap reserve. Reduced to a few hundred by disease and by war with the Comanche, these survivors had found shelter in the dense growth of the forest, where the enemy's superior mounted tactics were useless. For the U.S. Cavalry, the Tonkawa made fearless trackers and occasional auxiliaries, always hungry for Comanche blood.

At his feet were the buckboard's familiar ruts cut into the powdery ground. Shodden hoofprints flanking them belonged to cavalry mounts, undoubtedly the animals lost in the station raid. To give Stardust some walking rest, Renald continued on foot. He soon came upon the first sign that the Comanche party had exited the pass without caution equal to his own.

A single arrow was sunk into the ground like a stake marking a claim. He lowered himself onto one knee and yanked it from the soil. The length of the juniper shaft and fletching indicated Tonk make. Its wooden arrowhead revealed flint had been lacking for tips. He ran the eagle feathers over his palm, scrutinizing the landscape. Did he have some renegade Tonk to fear as well? He stood, discarded the arrow, and pressed forward. Ahead, where a bed of prickly pear had been crushed, the parallel tracks curved to the right before arcing back onto the trail. Either the driver had swerved in a volley of arrows or, wounded, had lost control momentarily.

Renald's attention was arrested by a lance split over bloodstained ground. An impaled rider had fallen here, but no corpse remained. That the body had been removed like hunted game was a sure sign of Tonk doing. The color and brittleness of the patch told him the attack had occurred yesterday. Hoofprints showed that the riders alongside the buckboard had attempted to scatter, but external pressure from both sides forced them back in line. He recognized the tactic used against them. The pursuers had approached at converging angles, affording easy side-shots for a tribe comparatively unskilled at firing from horseback. In officers' school this angled attack was called a *V* maneuver. Here, having charged down the ridge on fast and fresh mounts, the Tonk had employed it to wipe out their enemy in seconds.

Another dozen paces brought Renald to the site of the massacre. Here the earth was overturned violently in random accumulations of dirt and gravel. The horses had fought for footing, the men for their lives. Here, too, no bodies had been left to provide a seared feast for the creatures of the desert. What remained among the scattered patches of blood were headless broken lances and splintered arrows, the Tonkawa having retrieved everything of value while packing their booty. At this point the wheel grooves ceased their westerly movement and, digging deeper, turned abruptly northward. To Renald, the deeper ruts accounted for the extra weight of the deceased, piled high. He peered northward toward the treeline. A veil of smoke reached from there to the sky.

As he pivoted to mount Stardust, an unexpected flash of color caught his eye. Sprinkled with dirt, ruffled, a light-blue object lay practically at his feet. A piece of fabric? He reached down and promptly righted himself, slapping the material clean on his thigh. Attached, a label read *Cartwright's, Fort Worth*. He buried his nose in the cloth's fragrant folds. Acquired by trade, white women's scarves were prized by squaws. A brave, rich in horses, might trade for perfume too. But to find such an item among the remains of a battle between war parties was alarming. Beckert had thought the stagecoach held men alone. Could he have failed to notice a woman, or were the

Comanche already riding with a white captive? If the woman was now in Tonk hands, she was witnessing a celebration more terrifying than the slaughter. He looked westward, as if to say good-bye to his mission. The late afternoon glare registered only the odd silhouette—an outcropping here, a gentle rise there. Again he eyeballed the campfire smoke issuing from the forest. This time he heard the drumbeats. Shaking his head in resignation, he mounted up.

* * *

That the Tonkawa tribe worked with the army was no safeguard for a lone white man on the prairie, particularly one with a pack mule in tow. Approaching the forest, he caught sight of a handful of men astride dappled ponies emerging from the trees. Surely additional warriors were watching him from concealment. Renald might've waved his cavalry yellow neckerchief in the air, but only by taking charge could he obtain the woman.

A brave, center, raised his rifle. Together they kicked their horses into motion, war-whooping.

Renald could've reached for his Winchester—or turned tail. Most men would've done the latter, abandoning the mule. Instead, he crossed his hands and waited. Despite being denied the challenge of a chase, the Indians maintained a furious approach, picking up speed, intent either on striking or testing his mettle. Would he break? He sat firm, squeezing the saddle horn. The hoof thunder grew. Beneath him, Stardust stamped and neighed in trepidation. The low hanging sun cast a peach-like hue on the sinewy workings of the oncoming beasts and their bare-chested riders' quivering musculatures. Seconds more and Renald spotted paint on the men's faces and chests. At last, within spitting distance, they tugged their horses hard back, throwing powder in his face. The brave who had elevated his rifle to start the charge laid it across his thighs. Only he was mounted on a saddle, a *trooper's* saddle, but like the others he wore a breechcloth and a string of beads. His long hair was parted in the middle and sashed behind his shoulders. Without lifting his hand in greeting, he said, "Captain Renald …"

Renald blinked. "Retired," he replied.

* * *

After being recognized by the rifle-bearing Indian, a sometime army tracker whom troopers called Texas Tonk or just Texas, Renald was greeted cordially by the other warriors. One even offered a halting, "How you do?" to the amusement of his fellow braves. But friendliness in frontier relations could turn instantly to menace. They might not be so jovial when Renald produced the woman's scarf from his pocket.

Texas pointed to Renald's rifle. "Why you not kill us? Winchester shoot far."

Renald shrugged. "We ain't enemies."

The Indian crossed his bronzed arms. "But our cries … You not afraid?"

Renald appraised the six sweating warriors. "Nope."

A Tonkawa would never admit fear, either. The Indian's gaze wavered, then fixed on Renald's eyes again. "What you come for, Captain?"

"Comanche trail leads here. But they left their blood back there." He dug into his pocket, withdrew the shawl, and dangled it in the air with aplomb. "Give it a sniff."

The Indian prodded his horse forward and accepted the garment with a suspicious look. He held it to his nose while meeting Renald's neutral expression. This gave both men time to think. That Renald merely suspected a white woman had ridden with the Comanche wasn't obvious. For all Texas knew, he'd been dispatched to trade for her. If Renald rode away without the captive and reported the Tonkawa unwilling to acknowledge they held her, the army would march against them without delay. Yet if the tribe released the woman to him, Renald might claim he'd rescued her from them. They'd pay a heavy price for that too. Safer for the Tonk, Renald speculated, just to kill him and deliver their second-hand captive to Fort Sill or the closest outpost. They could eat Stardust to hide their crime, keep the mule and wares, and perhaps get something in the way of a reward. In all, a pretty good haul. But would the Tonk risk his murder? Renald wasn't as confident as he was bold. In any case, he presented a problem too big for Texas.

"You can't settle this yourself," he appealed, indicating the forest. "I want an audience with Buffalo Run."

Texas handed the scarf to the nearest rider. He joked in their language, "A gift for your wife. Tell her it's from Texas." Laughter followed, and he turned his horse toward the forest.

More sentries were posted at the tree line, perhaps guarding against a Comanche reprisal. The interior was dark and cool, and the ground was covered in fine pine needles. Nearby merrymaking could be heard—pulsing drumbeats, high and low toned chanting, and delirious imitation animal cries, all echoing in a cacophony through the timber. The clamor explained the war paint. Somewhere ahead, in ritual dance and song, the tribe was reenacting their bloodthirsty triumph over the enemy. Renald was told to dismount and picket his animals. A few minutes' walk brought him and his escort to a small clearing and the source of the racket. Around a campfire lounged a group of elders puffing on cigars and merrily passing the whiskey, while dancing at their backs was a ring of hooting, undulating braves in breechcloths, brandishing weapons. In all there were sixty or seventy men present.

When Renald stepped from the shadows with Texas at his side, the drummer lifted his palms from the antelope skin, effectively stopping the festivities. A hush followed. Such was Renald's notoriety that as he strode forward, the merrymakers, without being ordered to make way, fractured their line to reveal the inner circle of elders. He entered the breach and immediately recognized Chief Buffalo Run across the cook fire. The former fighting man appeared frail under a massive headdress. It was a wonder he could support it on that thin neck. Painted hoops made from bison bone hung from his elongated ears. To a man, the chief and his advisors were dressed in their finest—colorfully dyed cloth, buckskin tunics, and feathered headdresses. Far from showing signs of privation, their laps were filled with bowls of stew, the air thick with its smell. By this time, the blaze generated what light existed there while a gunmetal glow blanketed the treetops. No women were present, no living arrangements visible— the dwellings deeper in.

"Captain Renald!" called Buffalo Run.

Renald tapped the rim of his hat with two fingers, a casual gesture derived from the cavalry salute. Remembering the missing Comanche, he gestured toward the steaming pot hanging from a tripod over the flames. "Leftovers?"

Buffalo Run offered the army-issue bowl with both hands. "You hungry?"

"Not that hungry."

After a pause Buffalo Run asked if he'd come to trade—a safe, neutral question. Texas translated throughout.

"I wouldn't call it that. I've come to collect what's ours." Renald regarded the stew with trepidation.

The chief did not respond at first, heedful of the other elders' restless glances and whispers around him. At last he reverted to the *hókwat*, the white man. "Rest, Captain. Enjoy a smoke, a drink. Today we can show much hospitality."

Texas remembered. "The captain doesn't drink."

"Another time, Chief."

Buffalo Run frowned in the firelight.

Renald unbuttoned his shirt pocket and withdrew a twice-folded sheet of paper, offering it to Texas.

"I speak only …"

Turning back, Renald addressed the gathering. "It's a commission from General Sheridan charging me to trade for captives. The reward is three hundred dollars a head. The scrip's in my saddlebag. With it you claim your money. You can buy what you need right at the fort."

Animated chatter among the elders followed Texas' translation. One of Renald's guides approached the chief and whispered in his ear.

"And your mule?" asked Buffalo Run. "I'm told she is hauling goods for trade."

Renald restrained a smile. "I won't be needing those items if my mission is completed here. There's some pots, pans … knives, matches. But I do require the mule and certain essentials for the journey back."

The chief allowed himself a last mouthful before setting down his bowl and spoon. He got to his feet with effort due to age or whiskey or both, and somebody gave him a walking stick. Shuffling cautiously in his moccasins, he made for Renald around the circle. The elders followed his movements over their shoulders. Stopping chest to chest in front of the taller, fitter, younger man, he peered into Renald's eyes, still chewing.

Renald pursed his lips and wished he could close his nostrils. Buffalo Run's breath smelled meaty.

Without removing his gaze from Renald, the chief said, "Bring the captain's animals. The woman too."

* * *

Soon after, they produced her. A pair of old squaws flanked her emergence into the flickering light, undoubtedly wives of an elder or two. Wearing embroidered cloth gowns and beaded necklaces, they brought her before Renald and Buffalo Run only to retreat, eyes downcast, into the murky timber. Renald had expected somebody either squawified or hideous in her squalor and indignity—like other women he'd saved. Instead, dressed in a well-filled blue blouse and—man-style—in smart, tan saddle pants, she held her chin high, appearing scrub clean. Her shoulder-length blond hair glowed like embers in the firelight, and at her waist she clasped a hat.

Accustomed as he was to liberated captives crashing into his arms, spilling tears onto his shirt, he felt foolish here, his bravery mocked. He pinched the edge of his hat. "Pardon the observation, ma'am. But you look set for a riding lesson—not a rescue." Something was familiar about her.

She replied in a halting whisper. "They brought me here yesterday. The squaws washed my clothes and groomed me. I feared the purpose."

"Looks to me they treated you mighty fine. Let you eat too?" When she nodded, he pointed at the cook fire. "You eat *that*?"

She shook her head. "I couldn't."

He asked her name.

Eyes locked with his, she replied, "Shouldn't you introduce yourself first?"

"Should I?" He felt the focus of everybody's attention. With a hint of suspicion, he answered, "Scott Renald, army redeemer out of Fort Sill." He leaned forward. "Now, what about you, ma'am? Haven't we met before?"

Her gaze wavered and fell.

"You don't want to tell me your name?"

Again she didn't respond. Though it felt unfitting, given her tidiness and composure, he continued in a vein he was accustomed to. "Ma'am, if you've endured anything untoward, nobody's ever going to ask."

She shook her head.

He glanced at Buffalo Run resignedly. The old Indian was remote, too, as though he and the woman shared a confidence. Scrutinizing him, something drew Renald's attention. It was his staff. The firelight revealed a pair of bulges above and below his grip. Renald's curiosity captured Buffalo Run's attention, and the chief held out his trophy. Laced to the cane's head was a long-haired scalp. Stringy hair fell in clumps over his fist, while below it dangled a pair of clawing human hands, cinched together.

Renald swallowed.

She said, "He was alive when they did it."

Renald was taken aback. "Why should *you* be offended?"

Her sole reaction was to bite her lip.

Rescues were typically un-talkative, but this one was different. He tucked his thumbs behind his belt. "Miss, just what should I know?"

"Know?" She reacted with surprise, pointing at the steaming pot. "I'd like you to tell me what justifies *that*?"

He shrugged. "If I was a cannibal …"

"You think that's funny, Mr. Renald?"

His tone hotter than hers, he snapped back. "You figure Comanche raiders deserve a proper burial?" Then, "Just who are you?"

She sighed in capitulation. "I'm Miss Little."

His lips parted. "Miss *Little*?"

"Yes."

"Laura Little?"

"Yes. Laura Little."

"That seals it!" he growled. Over his shoulder he told Buffalo Run, "Now I understand why you held her, treated her right. Maybe she's worth more in horses! Well, I ride alone." He turned to locate his horse. His animals had been brought to the clearing's fringe where a brave minded Stardust. Renald marched over in disgust.

Behind him restless movement ensued. The elders began protesting. Finally Texas called out, "You don't want the woman?"

Renald took the reins in his left hand, slipped his boot into the stirrup and swung up into the saddle. "Far as I'm concerned," he replied, "you can eat her."

Several braves started for him. A raised hand from Buffalo Run made them halt.

As Renald swung Stardust around, Miss Little came running, tears coating her cheeks. With both hands she clutched his boot in its stirrup. "Take me with you, I beg you!"

He gave the night his attention. What should he do in this situation, with those Hermann boys still unaccounted for? Silence prevailed in camp.

"I'd be obliged if you'd unlock me," he told her.

She released him, reluctantly, and he stepped down off the horse. "You were no captive of the Comanche, Miss Little."

"Not this time," she replied, throwing her arms around his rigid body.

Over her shoulder he saw the men forming a crescent around them, their backs to the fire. Among them were Buffalo Run, Texas, and a brave with Miss Little's sash tied around his neck. After a moment, Renald separated himself from her and stepped toward the warrior, speaking in English and sign. "Give it back. The scarf, return it."

Miss Little protested. "Mr. Renald, no!"

The brave signed back. "I like the color."

She pleaded, "I don't need it!"

"A neckerchief has utility in the desert," he replied. "And that one's yours."

Renald extended his palm toward the Indian. In a show of bravery, the warrior reached for his knife.

Buffalo Run would have nothing of it. He intervened with a shout.

The warrior released his grip on the handle and dragged himself over to Renald. He stopped just inches from Renald's face. Behind him in the fire's glow, Texas repeated the chief's orders. Relenting at last, the brave tore the garment from his neck and thrust it forward.

Renald took it between his thumb and forefinger. Turning to Miss Little, he said, "Don't fret, I'll wring it clean."

She glared in reply.

"One more thing," said Renald, turning toward Texas. "What happened to those white scalps the Comanche were carrying?"

Texas pointed at the fire. Kindling for the dinner pot.

Thinking of Beckert, Renald said, "That's a kind of revenge, I suppose."

Chapter Three

When they were some distance south, traversing a luminous sapphire prairie beneath the full moon—a so-called Comanche moon—Renald drew rein. Behind him, the mule carrying Miss Little stopped in turn. "We'll rest here," he said in the Comanche language.

As if the rope between their animals connected their senses, too, he could feel Miss Little stiffen. "I speak English," she responded tersely.

He reverted to their mother tongue. "Safer to talk Comanche."

"Are you making fun of me, Mr. Renald?"

He nodded toward the forbidding terrain, all indistinct rock formations and night shadows. "Much birdsong tonight."

"Too much," she agreed.

He dismounted and helped her down from the mule. "Either Comanche bucks'll silence 'em or dawn will. Those Tonkawa will steer clear of where they spilt Comanche blood."

"Must you talk about that?"

"Talk about it? It's there we go east to Fort Sill." He looked at her differently. "Make no mistake, Fort Sill is where we're headed. You're my rescue." Returning to the mule, he added under his breath, "Damn shame …"

From the beast's load he retrieved his spare bedroll. He crossed in front of Miss Little and let it unravel on the fresh, hard earth. While she observed his movements back and forth he unlashed his own rubber trooper mat from behind his saddle, unrolled it a respectable three feet from hers, and laid blankets down for each of them. Dropping a canteen into the gap, he said, "Been an awful long day. I could sleep."

"We both should," she said, removing her hat and shaking down long, blond falls.

Unrigging Stardust, he pretended not to notice. "I confess I haven't got the reserves to sit watch. I'll thank you to resist the urge to night-ride him." He pulled off the saddle and heaved it onto a stone. "I reckon you ride bareback as well."

"I can shoot *galloping* bareback. But I won't steal your horse, Mr. Renald. After all, I don't quite know where I'm going."

"It's dangerous country if you don't," he replied.

"If you're confident in my riding, let me ride free at your side tomorrow."

He didn't react. Instead he finished his duties as if she wasn't there.

The suspicious birdcalls ended shortly thereafter, and the man and woman bedded down side by side, somewhat relieved. Renald's exhaustion was such he slept without regard to danger, or to her. Night passed. Upon waking minutes ahead of sunrise he rolled over to find Miss Little lying on her back wrapped in her blanket, pretty head on saddle, chest rising with each heavy breath. He sat up and enjoyed the starlit view a bit longer. Next, he squeezed into his boots and got to his feet. Standing over her, he prodded her shoulder with the stock of his rifle. Her eyelids fluttered open.

"You could cook some coffee," he said.

He built the smallest, most cautious of fires, and while she measured and boiled the coffee in a battered kettle he watered and saddled the animals.

In the still-sharp morning air they sat down together by the fire to drink from tin cups. Renald, facing west, remained silent. More than once Miss Little opened her mouth to speak before thinking better of it. Had Renald as much as glanced at her, he would've noticed her agitation. Instead he was captivated by the dark depths of his cup, held between gloved hands. At last she lost patience, erupting, "You all but told the Tonkawa to make a meal of me, Captain!"

With this she earned his attention. "Retired," he replied.

"Just where's the Southern gentleman in you?"

His face was hidden by the brim of his hat. "Maybe I should describe what your Comanche friends did back there before getting themselves gobbled up by the Tonk." Raising his steely eyes, he added, "Or did you see it yourself?"

She shook her head.

"Well then, one victim resembled a pincushion for all the arrows in him. Others were shot to pieces. The stationmaster was left alive, blinded, and pruned like a tree trunk. I had to mercy-shoot him. He was my friend, Miss Little."

She said nothing at first. Then, "My husband attracts the most violent youths."

"I'm not talking about him. I'm talking about the bucks you chose to ride with."

"I was kept back from what they did. When they brought me forward, it was over. They needed the horses."

"You needed one, too, ma'am." He sipped his coffee. "Why should I sympathize with a woman, once rescued by the army, who falls back in with the Comanche?"

"It wasn't a rescue—to me. I was taken captive, again."

He scoffed. "That's hateful."

"Is it? I recall the chase distinctly, Mr. Renald. I remember how the pony soldiers attacked at dawn when most of the braves, including my husband, were away. Attacked, I say, without warning. I remember women and children trampled by horses, jumping from rocks. I fought recapture." She spoke in a low voice for a woman and in a slow, careful way. Doubtless her English had come back since her repatriation, but she must have kept it in use during her captivity. She must've spoken English with a purpose.

"I heard you sunk your teeth into Trooper Tyler," he said. "That's sure gratitude, ma'am."

"Somebody was separating me from my son. I was struck on the head and awoke in the stockade."

"Those *I* rescue hug me, never bite."

She straightened. "I was less brutally handled by the *Indians.*"

He scowled. "Others ain't so fortunate. My rescues all endured hell and humiliation at the hands of Comanche bucks."

"I was held for marriage."

He swirled his coffee, his expression remote. "We don't always get the attractive ones back," he said, as if to himself.

She was about to speak, but instead took a pensive sip. Soon after, she broke her silence. "I was taken when I was sixteen. They told me my whole family died in the raid, which was a lie. Two winters later my son was born. When you bring a child into … another world … and the child only knows that world, and the squaws care for him as one of their own, eventually you accept the one world your son knows. And it's a good world for a child."

He nodded. "Much is said about Comanche cruelty, every word of it true. Yet nobody dotes over their children more. I've seen it myself."

"It's my life in Fort Worth I do not accept."

He regarded her fine garments. "Looks like you did all right living white again."

"I am still separated from my family."

"You mean your breed family," he said. "Men risked their lives for you, Miss Little. And your folks … now you've gone and disappeared again. That's the worst kind of loss."

"You say it as if you know it for yourself."

His critical look revealed nothing. "It's my business," he replied softly. "At least your boy saw what happened."

"Today my son is six years old. He hasn't heard from his mother in a year. The cavalry left him there like a stray dog."

Renald was unmoved. "If you hadn't behaved like a dog, you might've convinced them to bring him along."

Her eyes filled with tears. "I can't live with that. Do you understand?"

His gaze went beyond her shoulder toward the horizon. "I do."

"Mr. Renald, we're on the same path for the same purpose. There's little time before the army's autumn sweep."

Glancing aslant, he said, "Sweep? *Autumn*?"

"I know as much as you do—maybe more. And not from the Comanche."

"I believe it," he responded, "your uncle being the governor of Texas. He's why I'm taking you back."

"Kicking and screaming," she stressed.

"You'll ride back on your belly if you resist," he replied. "I got rope. Hold out your hands."

She slid back and tried another approach. "If we ride west together, I can protect you."

He chuckled. "Protect me, ma'am? Only if they don't shoot first. With a woman in tow, I won't pass for a trader. We'd look like some unlucky couple whose wagon busted. Easy prey."

"I might help you locate your rescues."

"Did I hear you say *might*?" He leaned forward. "We ride onto the Llano together, the Tonk'll come out after us, sure. The 10th will follow. If the Tonk don't find us first, I'll face an inquest."

"How do you figure all this?"

"I reckon those braves we heard last night were dispatched to Fort Sill. They'll be raging mad when they discover that army scrip's worthless. They'll be madder still if they're detained under suspicion."

"There's no reward in it for them?"

Renald scoffed, contemptuous of the tribe elders' naiveté in accepting his ruse. "It's payable only to hostile nations. The Comanche, the Kiowa, the Cheyenne ..." He reminded himself of the principal reason for keeping to his mission, possibly the last to be prosecuted in this country. Taking another good look at her, he couldn't help but acknowledge her immodest beauty, those wavy curtains of hair falling over the tucked-in blouse and those shapely thighs in tight pants. It was useless resisting her powers of persuasion. He tossed his coffee grit into the fire, rose, and glared down at her. "Ah, hell ..."

"Mr. Renald?"

"Best to take advantage of the chill, and the sun behind us."

"Behind us?" She lifted herself up. "Does that mean we ride west?"

He dipped his chin.

She threw down her cup and stepped around the fire. Though he tried to avoid her, she caught him by the arm and embraced him for the second time in a day.

Part II

The Staked Plain

Chapter Four

Gripping a rawhide horse lash, chin-whiskered Lieutenant Colonel John Davidson assumed his position before a wall-pinned map of Texas and Indian Territory. To his right stood First Sergeant Emanuel Chance, a solid black man distinguished by a thin mustache. At nine a.m. the interior temperature was still tolerable, and Davidson was decked out in his double-breasted blue coat and regimental cap. His staff had found seats around them in creaky chairs, on window sills, even on his own desk, from which a pair of sergeants dangled their long legs in yellow-striped trousers. The air was heavy with pipe smoke, yet hardly thick enough to repel the constant nuisance of horseflies. A kettle of coffee was being passed around. From knee to knee, somebody's glinting hip flask was making the rounds too. This was Fort Sill, Indian Territory, home of the 10th Cavalry. Assembled today in Davidson's office were four white captains, four black sergeants, some corporals, and the command's topographical engineer, all in their dark-blue shell jackets with yellow piping trim. The atmosphere was tense, the men exchanging whispers. "Black Jack"—as their commanding officer was commonly called, after the color of his troops—had just returned from a meeting of the regimental commanders at Fort Concho, Texas.

Chance called for quiet. His C.O. had led these men a long time, and while discipline in briefings was lax, there was no tighter troop on the march. Gaining the attention of most, Davidson gulped air and launched into his speech:

"As you know, despite internal divisions that prevented the ratification of the treaty of '67, Chief Iron Mountain of the Quahada Comanche ended hostilities last year, and Chiefs Bad Eagle and Wild Horse brought their bands in." He shoved the whip under his arm like a swagger stick. "But Iron Mountain is now dead, and his son Talking Moon has renewed armed resistance and violence against the settlers. Says he's had a vision …"

"Red Cloud had a vision too!" somebody yelled. "But them Lakota are tame today."

"Tame by a treaty that gave them the Black Hills," corrected Davidson, adding, "and only after they massacred Captain Fetterman. Seventy-nine soldiers lost." He cleared his throat. "Talking Moon knows treaties are made to be broken. To his followers, he's promising no less than the restoration of Indian medicine, immunity from bullets, victories over the army, the return of the buffalo, you name it. He's even imposed a traditional dress code on the Quahada. The consequences? You know them. All our posts are reporting reservation breakouts, raids, scalpings, and the inevitable abductions." He nodded to Chance, his top sergeant.

"Turns out," Chance continued, "it was Talking Moon besieged them hide men in Adobe Walls last month. And there was that incident reported down abouts Casas Rojas. Why, just last week he and his Kaiwa allies"—*Kaiwa* was Army for Kiowa—"ambuscaded B Company outta Fort Arnold, killing three troopers and making off with twenty horses and six repeating rifles."

Over the mutterings of his men, Davidson resumed his speech. "Consequences, indeed. The Texas forts have filled to bursting with terrified settlers. I saw it for myself at Concho, where General Sheridan convened a conference to address the army's response. He read us a two-item dispatch from General Sherman at St. Louis."

"Let's hear it, sir!" a sergeant called out.

Their commander set his feet. "Item one—by order of the president—all Indian agencies and reservations are hereby placed under army jurisdiction. That means it's our duty to register every last Indian in the territory and conduct periodic tallies. You will send word to the chiefs today that we start tomorrow, sunrise."

Predictably, groans and grumbles sounded from the men. One sergeant protested, "Sir, in our subdivision there's maybe twenty-five hundred plains injuns from three tribes to account for. Twice as many when it's inclement. Renegades winter here for army beef."

Davidson replied tersely. "Then we will have their names."

Chance intervened. "Following the lieutenant colonel's presentation, your captains will explain how it'll work."

"Men, listen up." Davidson tapped the whip in the palm of his hand while the room fell silent. "Item two—joint punitive action. A couple months back General Sheridan submitted a proposal to General Sherman for a large-scale invasion of Comancheria. Though we kept it under wraps, Sherman approved the campaign and appropriated the funds. Since then my counterparts and I have been amassing supplies and are today prepared to support troop movements on a grand scale. Your captains have been briefed and will fill you in this morning. The short of it is, we ride out Wednesday sunup, and we ride with celerity. No wagons. Just mules and buckboards."

Though a man or two cheered, a palpable apprehension filled the room. After all, the last hostile bands in dry country were the most determined of an enemy race that had, of late, held its own against regular troops. To march into their lands and pick a fight had few precedents, some with disastrous results. Ten years ago—at the first battle of Adobe Walls—an entire cavalry column was fought into retreat by fifteen hundred mounted Comanche. Two years later, in the worst disaster of the Indian wars, Captain William Fetterman's entire troop was annihilated by the Cheyenne and Sioux outside Fort Kearny, Wyoming Territory. Then there was Lieutenant Colonel George Custer's campaign against the Cheyenne on the banks of the Washita, south of Fort Sill. His recent book had framed it as a victory, but every horse soldier knew that twenty-one officers had perished there.

"It's war," somebody grunted.

"Maybe," Davidson responded. "The opposing forces are no longer sufficient to challenge one regiment, let alone *five*." He caressed his whiskers thoughtfully as the men echoed the number in astonishment. *Five* columns? "So," he added, "unless they're truly flapdoodle enough to believe their bare chests will deflect bullets, they'll attempt to scatter wherever we encounter them." He set one hand on hip and, fencer-like, lunged his improvised pointer at the map, indicating a place between the

Red River headwaters. "We believe the majority of the renegade Comanche, Kiowa, and Southern Cheyenne are encamped here … at the western edge of Palo Duro Canyon. To prevent them slipping into the canyon's labyrinth, the army will converge on the area from all sides—the biggest deployment ever in these parts." He turned toward Sergeant Chance, calling him by his nickname. "Tops?"

Taken by surprise, Chance sucked air. "From Fort Concho, Colonel Mackenzie's leading three columns north at a distance of thirty miles, with pickets spanning the intervals. From Fort Griffin, Colonel Buell is leading his column northwest. Major Price is marching east outta New Mexico, Colonel Miles south outta Kansas. As for our command, we wind our way northwest through the Palo Duro. That's three thousand men in forty-six companies."

Raising his voice over those of his now ecstatic officers, Davidson concluded, "The hostiles will flee with their families, their lodges, their food supplies, their ponies—but this time they will find no sanctuary! To quote General Sheridan, 'All segments of Indian society will experience the horrors of war as fully as the warriors.' " He paused. "This is the big one, men. By spring I expect to see wagon trains headed west from here, the door thrown open to safe settlement on a grand scale, courtesy of the United States Army."

The floorboards rumbled under stamping heels, the men hooting for emphasis. As the commotion died down, one sergeant put in, "While you was away, sir, smoke was reported in the vicinity of the Comancheria station."

Davidson looked grim. "I got the cable at Concho. A patrol will accompany the next stage from Fort Worth. If the post is found reduced we'll ride along as far as the Neutral Strip."

"If you please, sir, that stage ain't due for two days. We're worried about stationmaster Beckert."

"He knew the risks," replied their commander. "Should we start responding to every puff of smoke, the hostiles will use it as bait. Yesterday, Scott Renald rode out for the Llano in search of those Hermann boys. The station's on the way."

One non-commissioned officer sneered, "Johnny Reb Renald …"

Instantly, the group turned unruly again.

Davidson gathered himself. "You know I object to such talk. Like me, Scott Renald's a Virginian. In the late war, he elected to fight for his state. That hardly reflects the service he's done the country since."

"Or before," a black-bearded, Irish captain named Norton remarked to the men. "He served with distinction in Kearny's Army of the West."

"We fought the Mexicans all the way to California together," Davidson agreed.

"If I may, sir," said Sergeant Chance, "I'd like to remind my fellow junior officers it was another *Johnny Reb* treated us good after the 62nd was captured down at Palmito Ranch. That was Rip Ford paroled us alongside his white prisoners. So keep them *Johnnys* to yourselves!" His eyes darted from sergeant to sergeant. Then to Davidson, "Wouldn't Renald reverse direction to bring Sergeant Beckert back?"

Davidson drew a long breath. "If Beckert was found alive, I don't figure he'd be in any shape to travel."

The door budged open. From its frame a private saluted. When he lowered his hand, the young man seemed painfully aware of himself before his senior officers. Meekly he began to apologize for the interruption.

Davidson raised his chin. "At ease, Private …"

The young soldier took two steps forward, waving off some buzzing deer flies. "A mounted Tonkaway has approached the western gate, sir. Identifies himself as *Texas*. He speaks American, and he's riding army tack."

"If you were less green you'd know him," replied the lieutenant colonel.

Some laughed, the youth flushing.

Davidson eyed his captains. To a man they took Texas Tonk seriously. "Texas may be our best tracker," he told the private. "But I didn't summon him."

The young man squared his shoulders. "I thought the colonel would like to know, sir. He says it's about a Miss Little—Laura Little from Fort Worth. And he's waving a piece of paper."

* * *

Following the staff's dispersal, Sergeant Chance remained with Davidson, along with the commander's orderly. While Davidson's corporal saw to duties at his desk, the two men seated themselves on the shady porch out front, the senior officer having shed his button-down coat. Beyond lay the regimental marching grounds and barracks, empty now. A swarm of deer flies began their assault almost immediately. Pipe smoke would help repel them. Sergeant Chance had served under Davidson since the 10th was based at Fort Gibson, further east in Indian Territory.

Davidson struck a match, thoughtful of their exchange about Renald's treason and sensitive to having defended a former Reb to former slaves. The breeze carried flecks of tobacco onto his white shirt. "I can, of course, understand the men's sentiment about Renald," he offered.

Chance replied, "Like I said, I got no grudge against him. He risks his life 'fore we risk ours."

Davidson blew smoke. "Ever hear of Libby Prison?"

"Most everybody has, I figure. Some hellhole where them Rebs kept our officers."

"At Richmond," Davidson confirmed. "Well, over his C.O., Scott protested the conditions straight up to Jefferson Davis—and got demoted for it. So when President Johnson offered the Rebs amnesty to the rank of colonel, he was able to return to us, if merely as a scout."

"Same as Rip Ford," said Chance, cradling his pipe. "That's a lotta man to be kept outta the ranks." He tipped back his chair with his boot soles. "But that's sure where Scott Renald wants to be—roaming them plains, I mean. And this Laura Little, wasn't she a rescue?"

"Yes, from the Comanche. Trooper Tyler brought her in last spring while he was with H Company. Funny how that happens from time to time—long-held hostages being discovered in bands we've already traded with for hostages."

Chance combed his memory. "Ain't she the one Talking Moon took as a wife?"

"Bore him a child," replied Davidson through the lip of his pipe.

"She tried to get back to 'em, right?"

"Poor girl," said Davidson. "When they caught her, she cut her wrist. At Concho, I learned she broke out of the asylum they put her in. Tied up her doctor and borrowed his horse."

"That's justice!" said Chance in a burst of smoke.

"They found the horse, but not her."

Something occurred to Chance. He snapped his fingers. "While you was away a rumor sprung up ..."

Davidson motioned for him to continue.

"You know that old trooper, Cole Hawker—the hide man?"

"Hawk served with us in the Army of the West. Big fella."

"So damn big he sags his mount. Got hisself a tanning contract in Indian Territory."

Davidson nodded. "I awarded it to him. In return he reports what he sees on his hunts. What about Mr. Hawker?"

"The day you left for Concho he come back with his wagon stacked with tanned hides, claiming he'd glimpsed a white woman on the Comanche-Kaiwa reserve."

Davidson leaned in, raising his eyebrows. "Did he describe her?"

"Light of hair, nice figger."

"Miss Little is fair-haired. Did we inquire with the chiefs?"

Chance's pipe bobbed with the movement of his chin. "Yessir. But the corporals come back with nothing. Nobody seen or heard tell of an agency white woman."

"Of course they haven't! That would include one Millie Durgan. But we heard they were darkening her face with walnut oil. Could be, Laura Little joined that breakout a couple days back."

"But why'd she start out from here, not direct from Fort Worth?"

"I'd do the same, Tops. Just one coachway into Comancheria from here, little trafficked. No homesteads abutting. A station and its pen a day's walk." Davidson paused to relight. "She must've come through on the stage and slipped right over onto the reservation. Damn shame if she was involved in the station raid."

"Presumed station raid ..."

"I reckon Texas'll confirm it."

"He's always dependable," said Chance.

"And yet he's a little wild, isn't he?"

"Gives him an edge. Bunking here sets a scout at a remove."

Davidson screwed up his eyes. "That raid was timed in accordance with the coach schedule. Had to be. Without horses they couldn't stop it on the road … but stopped at the station it was an easy target. So the breakouts set out on foot in advance. I wonder how much she knew."

They drew on their pipes in pondering silence, awaiting Texas, shortly to be led around the quiet barracks and over the windswept grounds to them.

* * *

Flanked by an escort, Texas Tonk dismounted below Davidson's porch. Today he was dressed in yellow-corded blue cavalry trousers, trooper boots, and a simple white tunic. Leaving his saddle gun behind, he stepped up to Davidson and Chance, who received him on foot. Texas offered colorful salutations from Chief Buffalo Run. The first sergeant gave him a nod of familiarity and then checked him for weapons. Without remark, Chance unsheathed the knife from the Indian's belt and, pivoting around, planted it in a pine column at the stairs. Next, he gestured toward the troop commander's office.

Davidson's orderly met them all inside. Indicating a glistening silver pitcher on a stand beside his desk, the young corporal told the Indian to help himself. Texas didn't hesitate. He poured a tall glass and downed it. Davidson offered him a chair in front of his desk while perching himself on its corner. Just back of Texas, Chance clasped his hands behind his back, chest out. For his part, Texas was captivated by the survey map dominating the wall opposite them. Blue-flagged stick pins indicated the locations of forts; green ones, settlements; while other colors represented tribal enclaves, including his own and the Quahada's suspected principal encampment far to the west. Davidson pretended not to notice his interest. "I understand you've got information concerning the whereabouts of Laura Little," he started.

"I got other information too."

"Laura Little first," Davidson replied impatiently.

Texas removed a folded sheet of paper from his hip pocket and extended it to Davidson, his wrist dark and veined. The lieutenant colonel, grimacing, peeled the sweaty quarters apart. He snatched a pair of spectacles from his desk and examined the document. "Scott Renald issued this?"

"Yessir."

"I see." He removed the glasses. "How did Miss Little come into your possession?"

"She with Quahada," answered Texas. "Comanche burn station east of North Scalp, kill men. We kill Comanche." He grinned, adding, "Sheridan say only good Comanche dead one."

Davidson winced. "The general didn't say quite that. Just who did the Comanche kill?"

"Men in stagecoach. The whip, the shotgun too."

"And Beckert?"

"You know Comanche. They leave him die bad way. But he get gunshot to temple."

After a pause, "Do you suppose Renald charity shot him?"

Texas shrugged. "Man did it wear trooper boots."

The colonel rubbed his eyes. "They were old friends."

"Then Renald track Comanche through North Scalp Gorge ..."

Davidson imagined the rest. "Miss Little is as important to us as she is to Talking Moon. You didn't return her immediately. Why?"

"We ate."

Chance allowed himself a chuckle from his position behind Texas.

Davidson wasn't amused. "I would've expected Renald back by now. You rode ahead of him?"

"No. He go west with woman."

"*West?*" Davidson slid from his place.

"Yessir. Me and other brave see him and woman ride west. Brave ride back, tell chief. I ride here."

After a moment of visible disbelief, Davidson grimaced down at Texas. "You've always been a reliable tracker, even exceptional. That's why you've been rewarded beyond your pay … that saddle you're riding … But holding Laura Little overnight is suspicious. If you're lying …"

The cords in Texas' neck swelled as he looked up. "Why I lie?"

Davidson flapped the sheet of paper. "Maybe you forced Renald's signature before killing him. Maybe you sold Miss Little back to the Comanche. Maybe you're working both sides. I could throw you in the guardhouse till we've sorted it out."

The proud brave sprang up, chair crashing down, and met Davidson face to face. Chance disengaged his hands, just in case.

"You wrong, Colonel. Tonkawa your friend many seasons. We find Comanche for you, Kiowa, Cheyenne."

Davidson believed Texas—to a point. "And what about Miss Little? You found her too."

"But Renald take her!" He pointed at the scrip, still in Davidson's hand. "I want the money. Three hundred dollars."

"Texas, this scrip is invalid. We buy hostages back from the *enemy*. Let me remind you, we've already rewarded the Tonkawa for their alliance against the Comanche with repeating rifles."

"I not get money now? Then I kill Renald." He made for the door, kicking the fallen chair. Chance turned on his heels.

Davidson raised a hand, his brow furrowed. "You'll only get yourself scalped. Let's try another way."

The Indian stopped near the door and glanced sidelong at Davidson. "What way?"

"Sergeant, is Mr. Hawker still nearby?"

"Might be. I seen him about this morning."

To his orderly, Davidson said, "Find him."

"Yessir!" The youth jumped to his feet, grabbed his cap, and flew out the door.

Davidson returned his attention to Texas, righting the chair himself. "Are you familiar with the hide man named Hawker?"

"I know him, but I not like him."

"So?" Returning to the seat behind his desk, Davidson said, "I shall ask Hawk to ride after Renald. Other than Scott himself, he's the only person with a fair chance of survival in Comancheria. You'll escort him to the end of North Scalp Gorge, showing him everything you've seen, then cut out. If Hawk delivers Miss Little, I'll see you get something for it."

The Indian hesitated. "I return with promise, no more?"

"You tell Buffalo Run I'll reward him. I shouldn't, but I don't want Miss Little exposed to any more violence."

"Respectfully, sir …" Chance approached his superior and whispered, "If Texas goes back short the money, the woman, or Renald's scalp, he could wind up beef jerky. We can use him for the big one."

Davidson studied the wall map. He'd been trying to make Texas a regular scout for years, but the Indian preferred life in the wild. This time Davidson had some leverage. "Texas, what would you say to working with the pony soldiers again? You're already dressed for it and riding army tack. Under the Indian Enlistment Act, you get Lance Corporal and twenty-five dollars a month. I'll start you at thirty-five and Full Corporal with three months' pay to take back to Buffalo Run."

Texas looked disappointed. "Scout who work for Custer tell me he pay Bloody Knife seventy. Maybe I work for Custer."

"Well, go ahead! He's up in Dakota Territory."

Texas shifted his weight, saying nothing.

Davidson nodded, leaning back in his chair. "That's right. You're better off helping us clean out *your* enemy."

The Indian hesitated, suspicious. "What you need me for, Colonel?"

"I'll tell you once you're sworn in."

Texas pointed at the map. "I hear sergeant say *big one.* But that map wrong. Comanche closer than Palo Duro."

"They are?" Davidson stood. "Where are they?"

"Talking Moon in Double Barrel Gorge," came the response.

Davidson eyed him. It was impossibly good news. Still, "Indians avoid ravines same as us."

"Maybe that why. Be hard to get troops in and out alive."

"How many lodges?"

Texas shook his head.

"So you haven't seen the village yourself."

"No. But it where Comanche breakouts going. They tell us."

"I bet that was some dinner conversation," Chance quipped.

Davidson breathed in expansively. "That's what you meant about having *other* information …" He processed it in silence.

The entire operation would be modified based on this intelligence. He had to run the recommendation through General Sheridan, who, if willing to indulge the tip, would order the other regimental commanders to establish new, more easterly movements and forward communication points. Sighing, he warned Texas he'd better be right. "If you aren't, it'll cost me dear."

"Army must move quick before Comanche move."

"Oh, we will." He turned to Chance. "Tops, get me a detailed map of the place."

"Yessir."

Stepping eagerly to his orderly's desk and opening a drawer, Davidson told Texas, "The term of enlistment is two years. That means you'll go where the work is. You might wind up with George Armstrong Custer after all."

Chapter Five

A six-and-a-half-footer, bullnecked behind a stringy beard, the buffalo hunter Cole Hawker could've wrestled his bison down—or joined the herd himself. On and off the hunt he wore their hides over his rounded back and chewed tobacco like cud. His bristly person stank like he'd lain in a trough of whiskey, then rolled around in a cattle pen. A simple planter's son, he'd sought adventure in the west, enlisting in the cavalry in the forties and fighting Indians and Mexicans prior to his conscription into the Army of the Potomac, where he rose to first sergeant. Instead of advancing his military career after the war, he started hunting at a time when an enterprising plainsman could get rich off the great herds. Had he not gambled, drunk, and whored his money away, today he could be reclining in some hammock instead of chasing measly herds around Texas and tanning on the Comanche-Kiowa reservation. Same as many Texicans, whether Yankee or Reb in their sympathies, his career biography ran roughly parallel to Renald's, and like Renald he was a force of nature.

Casting a surprised glance at the Indian dagger pinned to the lodgepole outside, he slapped dust off his ragged hat and squeezed his untidy mass through the doorway. Davidson's lanky corporal stepped around him, offering water.

"Never touch the stuff where tongue oil can be found." In Hawker's resonant reply, one could hear the roominess of his great gourd of a chest. Acknowledging Davidson, seated opposite, he swatted dead a fly on his cheek. The pulverized bug slipped into his beard. To the left of Davidson's desk, Sergeant Chance stood with Texas Tonk. The Indian was peeling bills.

Consulting the clock—it wasn't even ten—Davidson reached below resignedly and opened a drawer. He set down a small glass, rose, and uncorked a bottle of sour mash. Cole Hawker swaggered forward.

"I see Texas Tonk is back!" the hide man boomed in a voice rough with prairie dust. Disregarding Sergeant Chance, he nodded at Texas, then jabbed a finger at the map. "And I recognize what each of them flags represents. Forts, camps, reserves, and known wild enclaves. Seems to me, I brought in some of that injun intelligence myself." He squinted. "But what's that 'un *there*? The red flag in Double Barrel Gorge …"

Davidson held out the drink. "Texas thinks Talking Moon's in there."

Hawker accepted the whiskey with a look of surprise, even concern. "That's damn close to the Tonk Forest, ain't it?" He downed half the pour.

"And from there not much farther to us," added Chance.

Hawker finished his drink with a guzzle and thumped the empty glass on the desk, suggestively. "Gets me wondering if that sweep we been expecting is closer at hand. Is it?"

"I summoned you for something else, Hawk." Davidson poured him another. "I suppose you've heard speculation the Comancheria station is gone."

"Speculation? I reported the smoke. Saw it from Split Rock Ridge."

"That so?" The lieutenant colonel sat down. "You have my thanks."

"A good man, Beckert. Fought bravely with us in Mexico."

"Texas here reports him dead," answered Davidson. "He thinks Renald charity shot him. I think so too."

The retired trooper lowered his chin. "They like us to die slow." He knew the Comanche, friendly in times of trade, sadistic in times of war. As if the Indian scout wasn't present, he continued, "How come Texas reported it? Did Renald leave the body fer the buzzards?"

"He pursue band through pass," answered Texas, grasping the envelope stuffed with bills. "We Tonkawa get revenge first."

Hawker raised his tangled eyebrows. "Rangy kill. I'd rather eat antelope."

Davidson ignored the impertinence. The men were always making fun of the Tonkawa's practices. The Tonk were grudgingly used to it. "That's not all," he said. "Apparently Laura Little was riding with the Comanche. Scott found her in the Tonk Forest."

Hawker whistled. "Laura Little! I thought I seen an agency white woman, told the quartermaster."

"You have a scout's eye," said Davidson, admiringly.

"I got eyes fer a nice figger, and she sure got one."

"Trouble is, Texas reports that she and Renald are headed west, not east."

The big man absorbed this. "She's worth a bunch to Talking Moon ..." He swung toward Texas. "That why you Tonk was holding her?"

Texas said nothing.

Revolving back to Davidson, he continued, "Maybe Renald hopes to trade her fer other captives."

Davidson shook his head. "I can't see Scott trading a white woman back, even if it's her will—the governor's niece …"

Chance shared his superior's skepticism. "He wouldn't do that."

Hawker huffed. "Him riding into Comancheria with Laura Little, the outcome'll be the same whether Talking Moon allows him to trade fer her or not. That Miss Little sure has pluck slipping onto the reserve and joining a breakout party. Takes nerve and more." Again returning the glass empty to the commander's desk, he ran the back of his hand over his lips and beard, exposing a coarse, dirty palm. "You got some problem, Black Jack. Judging by the stock-up I been witnessing, punitive action must be just around the corner. But now *little* Laura Little's run off onto the battlefield with yer *big* Comanche expert. Woo-wee! Has Scott lost his head?"

"What if he's really gunning for Talking Moon?" said Davidson.

Hawker thought it over. "You mean by using the woman to get close?" He shook his scruffy head. "Where'd that leave him getting back? Pure suicide."

"Scott's a lonely man, Hawk. And he owes the Comanche something."

Hawker thumbed his belt. "Doesn't mean he'd throw his life away fer a good cause. Take it from another lonely fella. But you didn't call me in to chew the fat. You need somebody tough enough to deal with Renald. Somebody who knows the country, who stands a chance of coming out with the woman. There's only one man qualified."

Davidson restrained a smile while Hawker grinned so broadly his missing teeth became countable. Though Hawk's appearance was beastly, Davidson knew that under all that matted and wiry hair, bison hide, and desert powder was a man as handsome as the ladies' favorite—the slim, blue-eyed, pale-haired, and singularly clean-shaven Scott Renald. The lieutenant colonel leaned back in his chair and pointed at the twice-emptied glass in front of him. "I need better than bottled bravery."

Hawker rested his boulder-like fists on the desk. "Gotta ride light. The bottles stay here. Ain't no whiskey mills out there."

"Think you can overtake them?"

The hide man regarded Texas. "She riding her own mount?"

"Mule," said the Tonkawa.

"Then they'll rest little." Hawker sighed. "Well, let's hope his horse fails."

"Not likely—that's some animal," said Davidson. "But supposing you catch up. What then?"

"Well … I can deal with a resistant woman on account of my not being a gentleman, but what if Renald ain't inclined to stand aside?"

The colonel shut his eyes, imagining a showdown between the two men—Hawk was a monster but Renald was fast as a gunhawk. Davidson rolled up his heavy lids. "Before setting out you'll swear an oath to act in the interests of the United States Army. That includes serving Renald a sealed letter from me. I don't want you taking an easy shot at him from a distance—as you would a buffalo."

"Kind of you to trust me," Hawker responded. "Maybe I'll take that shot *after* serving yer letter."

"Your commission is to find and return the missing, not kill one to grab the other. Frail of mind she may be, but Miss Little's an adult responsible for her own actions. As for Renald, I don't have to remind you he's a valuable asset."

"He ain't gonna be one in prison," said Hawker. He rubbed his thumb and index finger together in the air. "Now, how much? Taking into account my losses …"

Davidson glanced amusedly at Texas. "You two got something in common." Then to the hide man, "Minimal losses, I'd say, given the herds these days and the distance you must travel to find one. But I'm willing to talk money." Conscious that Texas was consuming every word, he asked Chance to escort the Indian to the porch. The sergeant closed the door behind them, and Davidson addressed Hawker in the darkened room. "I'll compensate you for your time and risk, not for lost business. Remember, you're a patriot and a veteran. In this case General Sheridan must approve the offer. With luck, I'll get a response by telegraph within the hour."

Hawker stuck out his whiskered chin. "I want a ten-year exclusive dispensation to supply the command with meat."

Davidson regarded him for a long, contemplative moment, hearing the breaths filling and escaping that huge chest. Then, "Smart to plan ahead. By spring I expect to open the country. Besides our needs, that means more natives in Indian Territory, a lot more. I agree to five years should you bring Miss Little back alive."

The hunter could not contain his grin. "Seems a job worth doing!"

Flashing him a critical look, Davidson attached his spectacles and scribbled something down. "Draw what you need from the quartermaster." He tore a page free and handed it to Hawker.

"When's the campaign planned fer?"

"All right, I'll tell you. Day after tomorrow." He gestured toward the wall map. "When Renald was sent out we thought the Quahada were encamped at the western edge of the Palo.

If Texas is right and Talking Moon has moved into the Double Barrel, it means Renald will ride long—as far as Survivor's Bluff, maybe. From there, he'd head north on the Staked Trail. Now, go get your supplies and be back here on the double. I'll have more details to share once you're signed on."

"*Yessir!*" Hawker saluted for the first time in years.

Halfheartedly, Davidson returned the gesture, his attention already transferred to the work on his desk. The big man barreled out.

When the door slammed shut, Davidson removed his glasses. To his corporal, he said, "There goes thunder to Renald's lightning."

* * *

The long shadows of late afternoon vanished into the descent of dusk. Gold-tinged cumulus clouds darkened over the gently sloping plain. The air cooled. From clumps of scrub brush came the nocturnal revelries of desert birds.

It should have been time to pitch camp, but without explanation Renald was pressing on. Riding abreast of her, he was uncharacteristically making conversation as well. "So, how'd you do it? Break out of the asylum, that is."

She turned in her saddle, blue shawl embracing her face under the hat. "I stole a horse and bought a seat on the stage to Santa Fe."

"Same line you raided a few days later. More gratitude."

"I told you, I had nothing to do with that."

"You weren't recognized on the stage?"

"Am I that famous? It was fully booked. I sat on the boot with the driver."

"What did you tell him?"

"That I was going to visit my husband at Fort Sill."

"Sounds reasonable. Stage gets in late. Under the cover of darkness you stole onto the reservation."

"Well, I needed a hat."

"Of course. And now you plan to rescue your boy. Think you can just steal him away?"

"Mr. Renald, you don't have any children—do you?"

Scanning the outlying topography, he replied, "No, ma'am—I don't."

"Figures …"

"Ma'am?"

Her mule shook its head, annoyed by flies.

"You might throw a bound woman over a saddle," she said, "but you can't drag a child kicking and screaming across the prairie."

"Can't you?"

Exasperated, she shook her head. "When the soldiers storm through, I'll be holding my son close."

"Good idea," he said. "The troopers will ride clear around you, fearing that bite."

She stiffened. "That's hardly amusing, Captain."

"The Indians still call me by my former rank but you shouldn't, Miss Little. I came back from the war a civilian. Had to …" He leaned on his stirrups, stretching his legs. "If I can't convince Talking Moon to stand down, maybe you can."

She sniggered. "Convince him to become an agency sheep farmer? I'm not even convinced it's the better way. Everywhere I looked I saw friends half-starved and dying of thirst."

With a tap he raised the brim of his hat. "You exaggerate. But it's a fact there ain't a herd of buffalo left in those parts and scarcely any big game. This year there's a problem of beef supply owing to the hard winter and your husband's stealing cattle for himself."

"They've got to eat too."

"They can have the beef the other way. But he doesn't want the agency Indians to get it that way, either."

"You think he's deliberately making things worse?"

"I know he is. He's trying to destabilize the agency system. The women and elders line up for slim government rations while the braves sulk."

She locked eyes with him. "Until they join him."

"But it won't work. None of it. The old way is gone with the great herds." He looked around. "Enough talk. We oughta hightail it from here."

Half an hour passed. They descended into a wide, still crater, the bottom of which was sheltered from the sundown drafts. The faintest glow remained above its rim, like that of a distant fire. Claiming the night as Mars had claimed the desert day, the silver plate of the moon offered enough light by which to pitch camp. Renald swung off his saddle. "Good place to pass the night," he said, coming round to Miss Little's mule. He offered his hand.

"Kind of you ..." She stepped off her mount and they found themselves standing chest to chest. If the hour had been earlier he would've noticed her blush. "We saw nobody all day," she stammered, "not a soul."

"Don't sound too disappointed," he replied, turning away. He began unpacking her animal.

She stepped aside, holding her mule steady by the reins. "You think the Tonkawa would track us this far?"

"I know they would."

"That's why we rode hard till dark?" she asked.

His silvery form hesitated in the moonlight. "Couple hours back, I saw a dust boil behind us. Could've been the wind, though."

Her voice cracked. "How far away was it?"

"Far enough. But we'll break camp before dawn."

She took it for granted they were being pursued. "Can we evade them? Can we afford to stop?"

Renald had thought it through. Although the Tonk could night track, following a two-animal trail by starlight was likely to lead them astray. He wouldn't do it, and he'd learned from the best. He'd learned from Texas Tonk. "Most I can do is earn us time," he responded, "keeping to the gullies, avoiding the flats where possible, crossing hard ground to throw them off." Hiding his certainty, he crouched and began hoof tying Stardust, a picket useless here. "If there's Tonk behind us, they're riding twice our speed. I'll have to kill 'em."

She searched his blank face. "How do you plan that?"

"Dry-gulch 'em, what else?" He rose, his irritation apparent. "Be the second dishonorable thing I've done the Tonk nation in as many days."

"They eat people, Mr. Renald."

"They eat *Comanche,* Miss Little. Seems to me, *as a white woman,* you owe them more respect. They spared you, bathed you, didn't even rob you of that ring you're fool-wearing on your thumb. How'd the Comanche behave when they took you at that tender age?"

She unfitted the mule's bit and pulled its bridle. "I said it wasn't like that."

"You did say it." Renald accepted the equipment from her, but not her story. The famous captive Ophelia Wheatman was notoriously unreliable about her five years with the Mohave. She too denied being raped. But she also denied being married and yet wore the marks of marriage on her face. "Maybe you got lucky," he said, "but what about the others?" When she didn't respond, he changed the subject. "You sure those braves you were riding with didn't reveal the location of the main body?"

Miss Little shook her head.

"Hell," he said. "If you knew, you wouldn't tell me. Last intelligence we got, they were encamped west of Palo Duro Canyon. There's water there, pastureland, and good communications with the Southern Cheyenne."

"They trade horses and stolen cattle with them."

"They trade in stolen persons too, Miss Little. You of all people know that. They're back to raiding settlements down along the Pecos and the Colorado. Took two German boys."

"Sure it was Comanche?"

"The boys were easy targets, out in the corn fields scaring birds away. Never came home."

She shook her head and gripped Stardust's bridle unnecessarily as Renald loosened his trappings and unstrapped the girth. With the back of her hand she massaged the beast's flat, broad muzzle. Even at sundown his almost serpentine eyes sparkled. Stardust responded with an affectionate nibble and pushed forward into her. "Easy ..." whispered Renald.

"Were you sent out for those boys?"

"Yes, ma'am. 'Nother scout was sent into Apache land from Fort McKavett."

"They could be in anybody's hands by now. What if you can't find them?"

"I can ride back with any *taiboo* and satisfy my commission." He hauled Stardust's saddle onto a waiting stone.

Miss Little unrolled their bedding, first his, then hers, leaving less space between the mats than he had last night. Rising, she said, "Why don't you let me hold a weapon? I don't fancy the Tonkawa sneaking up on us while you nod off. You will."

He stopped to consider it, rubbing his eyes. "Comanche rifle trained you, did they?"

"If I weren't afraid of somebody hearing, I'd prove it," she said, "even in this light."

He drew his saddle gun from its boot and stepped close to her, extending it stock first. "You just won yourself first watch. Good night, Miss Little."

* * *

Reliably, Scott Renald awoke after a few hours. Lying on his back, wool-wrapped, for a few moments he gazed aloft at the glittering heavens and contemplated the bloody promise of the emerging day. The empty distance between themselves and their pursuers had become negligible. When the sun had risen high enough to cast westward shadows, painted riders would surely appear along the sawtooth rim of this stony bedchamber; but by then Renald would have found his striking place ahead.

Somewhere to the south a nightingale sang.

He heard Miss Little breathe out, doubtless impatient for her watch to end. Together they were sharing yet another starry evening, far from everything but danger. Raising himself on his elbow, he furtively admired her, as he'd done last night. This time, straight-backed and oriented eastward, she sat cross-legged on hard ground to keep herself awake, the rifle bridging her thighs. Her chest rose and fell. He waited for the movement to gracefully repeat itself. Other men could be tempted, but not Renald. In fact, this brief thrill led him right to gloom. Dealing with chance reminders of his loss was like maneuvering around some unexpected depression in his path. He dismissed this one by rising to his feet with such agility that Miss Little swung the rifle.

He stood before her like a monument in the moonglow. "I could've filled you with lead," he said.

Lowering the barrel, she moaned, "How romantic, Mr. Renald ..."

She reversed the position of the gun and returned it to him. They traded places, she dragging herself onto the bedroll and collapsing face down into slumber. Meantime he pulled the kettle from the dying campfire and poured himself some tepid coffee. Glancing here and there, he spotted a perch from which to keep a lookout for the uninvited while keeping an eye on Miss Little. It was a short climb up a boulder slide that ran down the basin wall. Balancing his tin cup in one hand and holding his rifle by the magazine in the other, he stepped from stone to stone, all shiny and shadowed under the stars, until he reached the place. He leaned the Winchester a grab away and lowered his seat onto a flat, night-chilled piece of shale. From this position he could hit any silhouette that appeared above, while remaining all but invisible himself.

Swishing his coffee, he found himself haunted by the memory of another time he'd taken the watch in hostile country, a full moon glowing as now. To settlers, a Comanche moon brought the threat of raids. On that unfortunate occasion, nearly a quarter century ago, his unit was pursuing raiders miles northwest of Camp Worth. Lacking a scout's guidance, they got lost while the warriors slyly doubled back to raid another homestead. At dawn Renald and his unit saw smoke rising southeast of their position. They returned too late. Renald was abruptly alone in life.

He felt a sudden chill. With a frustrated flick of the wrist he tossed the coffee grit.

Like a shotgun blast, the expulsion fanned in the face of someone springing from a black recess between two boulders. The clatter of dropped flint broke the silence. Startled and disarmed, the brave staggered back, clawing his eyes with both hands. Renald, after a moment's surprise, dropped the cup and made for the fallen knife. Holding it like a garden spade, he swept it upward between the Indian's elbows and plunged it into the soft flesh of his neck. The spurting wound was fatal, but a quick second blow was required to preserve the silence. He planted himself at his attacker's side and drove the blade deeper against the brave's panicked grasps. Then, clutching the Indian's scalp with his free hand, he toppled the man backward, cracking his skull on a stone.

Now Renald recognized him. It was the brave who'd fancied Miss Little's scarf. Renald had killed him quick and quiet, but the dual clangs of the fallen blade and cup had exposed his position. Indians never stalked alone. Another brave would have heard the alarm. He'd be coiling for attack too. Renald turned full around and threw himself toward his waiting rifle. This time a body leapt out of the darkness from above. Falling short of Renald, the fringed figure landed chest first in the dirt, expelling a defeated grunt. One hand clutched the ground, the other a dagger. Spitting dirt, he began getting up.

Again Renald resisted the urge to draw his weapon—a gun's cry would alert every Indian for ten miles. With his bloody hand, Renald grabbed the rifle by the muzzle. Using it as a club, he wheeled around and side-smacked his rising opponent, stunning him. Then, changing holds, he butted him full in the face.

The brave splayed lifelessly onto the other corpse.

Renald could not afford the luxury of a restorative breath. For all he knew, there were one or two more men out there in the darkness, possibly cat-footing toward Miss Little or their animals. From where he was she looked undisturbed, still in slumber. Left of her were their mounts in standing rest. In the moonlight, Stardust's flaxen mane and tail glowed. Renald propped his rifle against a boulder while he unfastened his second attacker's knife belt. He returned the weapon to its scabbard and strapped the belt across his chest, dagger forward. On his way back to Miss Little he chose his steps cautiously, lowering himself from foothold to foothold. Each crunching step seemed to shout out his location. He felt eyes on his back, imagined knives noiselessly slipping from sheaths, bowstrings tautening.

He found Miss Little just as he'd left her, face down on the bedroll. Allowing her to doze a bit longer, he rinsed his bloodied hands in canteen water, put the leather on his animal, and packed his bedding. He paused, suspecting he'd neglected something … but what? … A task? … An item? … Glancing around in the night hush, rubbing his palms against his waist belt, he remembered. The tin cup on the boulder slide, lying near the killed. No mind, he and Miss Little could share the other.

With vigilance he surveyed the entire perimeter of the basin, some fifty feet above, his hearing more acute than his sight. The moonlit surfaces offered no sounds, no movements. But that meant nothing. He dropped to one knee beside his ward and prodded her shoulder. "Miss Little … Miss Little …"

Nothing.

Louder in her ear, he called her name. He jostled her shoulder. Even after rolling her onto her back she continued to doze, her pearly face wrapped in the shawl, reflecting the stellar serenity. He exhaled in exasperation. No sense risking an arrow in his back yelling in her ear. He loosened his trooper's neckerchief, sprang to his feet, and took a canteen from the mule. A turn of the flask moistened the cloth, and he laid it over her eyes. Pressing it gently to her sockets, he repeated her name. Dribbles ran down her temples, and she began to stir. He plugged the canteen and waited.

Her eyelids fluttered. "Scott?" she murmured.

"Laura ..." he whispered, "we gotta mount up."

"Now?" she asked.

"Yes, ma'am. This instant."

A moment's intake followed before the message registered. Miss Little struggled to get free of the blanket. "What's happened?" Then, pointing at the dagger straddling his chest, "Where'd you get that!"

"Picked it off a dead Indian," he replied.

Her eyes widened in astonishment.

"I'll get us back atop," he continued. "Enough gleam to ride by, thanks to that Comanche moon of yours."

She shook her head with fatigue. "I took first watch, Mr. Renald. I can't have slept long. Minutes ..."

"Minutes count for hours."

"They'll have to ..." she sighed, rising.

She dusted off. While she rolled and packed her mat and cover, he emptied the kettle over the campfire remains and kicked sand on top. He assisted in lashing her saddle and helped her onto her animal. Then he mounted Stardust and moved them westward. The breeze chilled.

He led them clockwise around the arena, hugging the steep walls. Stardust proved himself a sure step in these conditions, a welcome surprise to Renald, who'd never tested him at night thus. They followed the bend of the basin. Renald kept his eyes on its luminous edge, his stone-like chin catching the moonlight. He halted at the narrow opening of a runoff trail. A funneled gust indicated it ran to the top. At bottom, the soft sediment wash promised a muted start. He ran his fingers through the white blaze of Stardust's mane. The downdraft would carry their scent. Their tracks would show. Yet they had to risk it. He ordered Stardust into ascent, Miss Little following closely on the mule.

It wasn't long till she broke their silence, whispering, "You hear that?"

"I did," he replied softly, still focused ahead.

"Any idea what it was?"

"Yep. Somebody toed my tin cup back there."

She gasped. "Scott!"

"Least we know there's more of 'em close. Better to know."

With his right hand he reached behind himself to place his palm flat on Stardust's rising and falling haunch. Shifting in his saddle, left boot pushing the stirrup down, he raised his seat to allow a backwards glance at Miss Little. Despite her tiredness, she rode her mule with dignity and poise in her shawl and hat. "We oughta hightail it," he said. "You fit to hold your mount?"

"Sure am," she answered. "Are you?"

He turned back with a smile, pressed his heels to Stardust's sides, and jogged his reins. The powerful creature lunged forward, instantly leaving Miss Little and her mount in the dust. She cast a wary look over her shoulder and expressed herself with her heels. The animal pushed ahead, straining.

For long minutes they drove their mounts uphill at a strenuous pace, the pack mule making less noise than before, much of its load left in the Tonk Forest. With an open, sympathetic hand, Miss Little smoothed over the sweat on the animal's shoulder and registered her labored breathing. Finally, where the dry gully began to level off and its roughened granite wash floor became treacherous to the horseshoe, they slowed, their steps on the rubble clanging as if made on broken porcelain. Here the path widened to allow side-by-side riding, and Renald held back for Miss Little as dawn began to break blue.

* * *

With sunrise, their night ride had led them to the baked flatlands of the Staked Plain, devoid even of spiny cholla or the sparsest scrub. Here, centuries ago, Francisco Coronado had used bones and piles of cow dung to mark his way, and those who followed him sunk iron stakes that could still be found today. The morning light pushed their shadows toward a remote low-lying butte, a boat at sea in the morning haze, remarkable in its lonesomeness.

"Survivor's Bluff," he observed. "From there we head due north."

A cool draft ruffled their sleeves and tingled their cheeks. Should they ride straight for the butte? Could they make it across? He weighed this against that. From some bird's nest atop that eminence he couldn't miss his pursuers as they crossed the plain. The range of his Winchester far exceeded that of their old Henrys. Or he could hang back right here and, point-blank, gun them down as they exited the gully. But would the Tonk fall for their own stratagem against the Comanche? And where would Miss Little be better situated should he fail and perish? At least on the butte she would be that much closer to their destination. The chance was remote, but maybe Talking Moon had posted sentries there to guard the approach. Reaching the rock would take an hour, maybe more, under a tolerant sun. Renald considered Miss Little's condition. They'd been riding nonstop.

She was wise to his concern. "I can manage it."

"You'll have to," he said. "We'll make you a comfortable bed yonder."

"Before you finish them off?"

"That's the idea."

"Can't I help?" she asked.

Predictably, he grew short. "Wouldn't you like to," he said. "We're burning daylight." He tilted his hat back toward the sun and chirruped Stardust forward.

Chapter Six

"There!" He patted the bed he'd made for her in a small cave beneath a granite shelf. Rising, he minded his head. "Should be satisfactory—you're used to sleeping on the ground, after all."

From under the brim of her hat, she flashed him a look. "I don't accept closing my eyes while you're risking your life."

"There's no telling how long we'll wait for a sign of 'em. Best you take advantage." He rested a hand on the butt of his six-shot. "In case you spend the night alone, there's a tin of beef next to your bed, and an opener and fork. Some jerky and hardtack too."

She swung into the cavern, lowering herself onto the mat.

"Cool in there, eh?" he asked.

She nodded resignedly, wearily. "I could put my head down, I guess."

"You *should*. You can slip in even deeper, out of sight."

She regarded the dark recess behind her.

He yanked a canteen from the mule. "Make it last," he said before turning away.

"Will you leave me unable to defend myself?"

He stopped. "They get past me and find you, don't fight. They sure won't be kind this time, but your value will save your life."

"I demand a weapon."

He saw the determination in her eyes. "Not smart," he replied.

"I know what I'm doing."

"Sometimes I think you do. More than you're willing to tell."

"I could gain time with one," she added. "And make noise."

"Suit yourself," he said. He dug into the mule's *aparejo* and retrieved a coiled gun belt. Placing it with her, he explained, "It's my old service Colt, meant as a deal sweetener." He dug his hands deeper into the bag and withdrew a short, white box. Shaking it, he added, "Take these." He found two longer boxes containing .44-40s and stuffed them into his pants. Pockets bulging, he began wiping traces of their footprints from the sand.

Watching him skeptically, she said, "Maybe the wind will do the rest …"

Renald shrugged. "Worth a try."

He back-stepped to Stardust's stirrup and, gaining a footing, lifted himself into the saddle. "I'll hobble the animals up over that ridge a ways where you can't miss, then double back and find a lookout. I'm trusting you won't ride away when my back is turned. We're in this together, Miss Little."

Her face was ashen. "I'll wait for you, Scott."

"Be cautious," he said, "but don't wait too long. If you ride out alone, leave at dawn and leave the mule behind. She'll be useless in a speed contest. Down there, observe close, and you'll find Coronado's old trail north, every so often marked with rusty stakes. Half a day's ride'll put you into Palo Duro Canyon. Ever seen it?"

She shook her head. "We used to follow the herds closer to the Colorado."

"The land opens like a gaping, red scar. It's a big, rough place, and it's anybody's guess where they're holed up in it. You could die in the looking."

"That's a comforting thought."

"I'll leave essentials with Stardust."

She studied him. "If we don't meet again, I'll always wonder how you came to call him that. Such a romantic, dreamy name. You don't seem a man given to daydreaming."

"I don't? What do you think I do in this saddle all day?" He paused. "Time comes, it'll sit you well."

Blushing, she replied, "Thank you, Scott. I'm sorry for this."

He pinched the brim of his hat. "*Nu supanaitu unu.* I understand you better than you figure." Renald swung Stardust around and left her holding the canteen like an infant.

* * *

He settled into some shade at cliff's edge, supposing the enemy would wait for sundown to cross. A distant fringe of brown marked the basin from which he and Miss Little had risen earlier. Waves of heat ribbed the mesa air.

Renald, who smoked solely for peace, had only his thoughts and memories to occupy him that long and lonely noontime. As if in mirage, he witnessed his life play out on the vast, empty stage. His first western posting—the Mexican war—the arrival of his wife by stagecoach—the homestead they built—the massacre of his family—the Indian wars—the Rebellion— and finally his perpetual what-if searches into these untamed lands. The event of his personal tragedy was a true exercise of the imagination because, when it happened, he was chasing its perpetrators in the wrong direction. Hence, till today, rather than struggling to shut out bitter memories, he would backslide into recreating that grisly scene in his head up until he discovered the remains.

On this occasion, he didn't linger among the collapsed rafters, smoking embers, and the blackened skulls that greeted his arrival too late. Instead he moved his thoughts to the future. If he survived the showdown with the Tonkawa and found the Quahada Comanche where they were supposed to be, tomorrow he could well deliver Miss Little into the arms of husband and son. For her return he would appeal for information on those recently lost boys. Only rescues could save him from disgrace. But, as Laura Little had warned, Talking Moon wouldn't let him ride out to betray his location to an army on the march. If news of the campaign had already reached the chief, death— not captives—could be Renald's reward.

For a time a talkative brown thrasher hopped inquisitively from stone to stone around him. As afternoon wore on, the odd coyote cry kept him alert. Out there, the butter yellow of the mesa darkened into honey gold. Then came the greys. While he could still see far, Renald cautiously scanned the monotonous, windblown horizon for movement, detecting none at all. Had disaster been averted? The Tonkawa might've followed much closer than this. Yet it was too early to let down his guard— north of the butte was nothing but tableland for hours.

Night settled upon the land and a wind rose and whipped around him among the broken stones. He stretched and pinched himself to stay awake a while longer, wondering persistently how so vengeful a pack could allow themselves such an abundance of time in enemy country. Were his pursuers passing a pipe around a campfire, opposite, while he fretted and resisted fatigue? Maybe. They might suspect this trap, guessing he'd abandon it ahead of dawn to press on. If so, rested, they could bypass the butte to gain time and overtake him on that wide open country. Whatever happened, Laura Little's worth was her guarantee of survival. If she fell again into Tonkawa hands, they'd either demand a trade with their rivals—maybe even a truce—or return her to Fort Sill.

Renald managed to keep himself alert for another two hours. When, ultimately, he felt himself succumbing to exhaustion, he began eyeing a hackberry bush opposite. By fashioning one of its spiny stems into a collar and lashing it to his neck, he could last all night, but that would leave him sapped tomorrow. With his last waking breath he unrolled his mat and fell into immediate slumber.

The night passed peacefully.

Arising before sunup, he felt remarkably refreshed—if stiff and hungry. Strips of jerky were his meal as he peered into the starlit expanse, the silence soothing. He wondered how Laura Little was faring, a woman left alone in a harsh and forbidding place, the promise of gunshots a specter. Straying in his mind from his immediate circumstances, he found himself in the itinerant Comanche camp along the Colorado where she was recaptured. He pictured her raising her little Indian boy in some dark lodge. He saw her sharing a mat by the fire with his father. He saw Talking Moon ransacking settlements, emptying livestock pens, scalping the men, and shoving distraught women and girls onto horseback. Renald remembered Talking Moon's father, Iron Mountain, with whom he'd traded for captives in better times for the tribe, and under whose leadership red-on-white raiding had declined. The old man's memory had stretched back to when the Comanche, numbering in the tens of thousands and rich in horses, dominated dry country. Unlike his volatile and reckless son, Iron Mountain had been a pragmatist who, though he refused to sign the treaty of 1867, which set aside the reservation lands, nevertheless ended hostilities and ceased the practice of taking captives, forbidden in Article Eleven.

As sunrise removed the blues and purples and peaches of dawn, he caught sight of something out there. Or did he? Renald rubbed his eyes and blinked, straining to keep the speck in focus. Was it merely a trick played on the eyes? Maybe. But he could swear the blemish was growing bigger. Stupidly, he'd left his spyglasses on Stardust. Minutes passed in which the distant thing grew and grew, a kind of ink spot rolling toward him over the plains. Gazelle? Antelope? Buffalo? Or was it the feared alternative? If animal in nature, the movement of the herd was unlikely—straight and determined as it was. To avoid losing focus, he trained his rifle sights on it, lowering the barrel gradually as the object came forward. Minutes more and it stretched into a distinct strip against the pale-rock desert floor, doubling in width, the landscape's backlight burning through its silhouette to reveal an irregular, bobbing crest. From the unbroken line, intervals appeared—one after another, creating three segments, now six, now nine. Finally in that notched pattern Renald could count the jouncing warriors riding abreast.

At most he'd expected two or three more braves to lay pursuit. Not near twenty.

Renald blinked sweat from his eyes and pushed his hat back on his head. This time he couldn't rely on luck to make the difference. Yet again, he should've been smarter. That dust boil he'd noticed two days back was kicked up not by a few warriors riding hard, as he'd thought, but by many riding confidently behind advance scouts, those he'd bested yesterday. This party must've left camp before dawn to hit the butte in the first useful light of morning. He squatted down. It figured Buffalo Run would send a redoubtable force deep into Comancheria. The Comanche themselves seldom rode in such numbers and didn't pack repeating rifles to a man. Still, the decision was poor. A capable shooter firing a repeater from a concealed place could be as deadly as a whole war party. It seemed the blood sought was worth risking the lives of all these braves, perhaps one-third of the remaining Tonk fighting men. Renald shook his head contemptuously, angrily. Pride ... honor ... what foolish emotions to afflict a nearly extinct people. They should be thinking of their survival. Nearly an hour since their appearance on the mesa, and with the sun risen high, colors began to emerge from the approaching line of warriors, including the white of a headdress.

Mad at them, at Miss Little, and at himself most of all, he guzzled water from his canteen. He set it down, detached fifteen rounds from his gun belt, and spilled them into a nook in the stone barrier that formed the edge of the cliff. He would surely need to reload—and fast. Therein was the Tonks' chance. He shouldered the rifle again and jerked the magazine full, then aimed. Licking his lips, he targeted the leader. Could it be Buffalo Run himself? That would explain the party's slow pace. They should've set out earlier. He allowed himself a long draw of scorching air. Laws did not exist out here, and the presence of a war party closing in on his position could not be misinterpreted. In his mind, he was already defending himself in a court of inquiry. These were, after all, allies of the United States Army.

Despite his respect for the chief, there was nothing more demoralizing to the enemy than its leader going down first. He pursed his lips and squeezed off a round. A moment later the distant figure went backward over his horse's rump. Spooked, the animal darted forward, kicking the fallen man to pieces. By then Renald had already dropped another brave, farthest right. Hoots and hollers erupted from the line as it broke into three segments, the center charging ahead, wings to the sides. He blasted two more braves farthest left. Now swinging right, he hit another warrior in the center, then dropped two others on the right wing. Next he stopped three more heading forward—they tumbled to the ground. In seconds he'd halved the Indian numbers.

Now he had to reload. The rest of the Tonk fighters scrambled to make cover while Renald, his back to a shielding stone, thumbed in ammunition. Riders from each wing drove their mounts toward the concealment of the rocky shelf while others in the center sprang from their animals to provide scattered gunfire. When he rose and pivoted back, his chamber half-loaded, the sight of these dismounted opponents confirmed them as Tonkawa—the Comanche would've fought expertly from horseback. He aimed again, firing rapidly. Two additional targets in the center toppled backward. Three others bounded over their bodies as Renald paused again to reload. In total only six braves got across. They would have to climb by hand and foot to his position.

On the battlefield the wounded squirmed in expanding pools of blood, too proud to groan. Their horses, loyal to their own needs, attempted to graze while drifting gradually toward the shade below Renald's position. The shade did not attract the injured fighting men. Instead, with their last breaths, they dragged themselves toward their unmoving leader. The sun would finish them off if they didn't bleed out first.

Renald had never witnessed such dignity in the fallen. In Mexico, in Virginia—in Tennessee—even the best of men had wailed like banshees after being smashed to bits on the field of battle, both from pain and fear of being overlooked among the dead. He ran his sleeve across his brow. Years ago, he'd witnessed with disgust passengers on the transcontinental firing into a herd of buffalo grazing along the tracks, dropping the beasts left and right. Today he'd similarly massacred honorable men, spilling their guts and brains onto the desert floor. But he could not allow himself to reflect further as he pumped rounds into his weapon. He must fall back. Feeling queasy suddenly, he nevertheless collected the empty casings scattered at his feet and shoved them down a crevice between boulders. Now, with the canteen slung, the rifle in one hand, and the coiled bedding tucked under his arm, he set out.

He made just a few steps before a sudden discomfort caused him to grip his belly. Low down, his guts churned. The rifle clattered to the ground, and he doubled over, hands on thighs. A deep-down release forced its way up. Irrepressible, it prised apart his gritted teeth, and he expectorated onto a flat piece of sandstone. The filmy, yellow material sizzled and smoked there. He coughed out the rest. Passing the back of his hand over his lips, he considered the consequences. Even if the sounds of his retching hadn't carried to the Tonk, the stain all but promised detection. He weighed the options, deciding to empty his remaining drinking water on it. In this heat it would clear in minutes. Yonder, Stardust's load included a full canteen. Renald licked his sere lips.

Restoring the rifle to his grasp, he scrambled over a rocky parapet like a tightrope performer, the sound of his footfalls caught by the easterly wind and borne toward his pursuers. As he negotiated the rocks he wrestled with what to do. He hadn't foreseen a situation in which both he and his attackers survived and he was forced to retreat. Should he draw the Indians away from Miss Little, he would turn his back on her and his precious water supply. If instead he withdrew to her position, the Tonk would certainly track him there, and speedily. Mounted escape wasn't an option. Her mule was worthless for speed, and Stardust, carrying two riders, couldn't outrun an Indian pony. After the Tonk had reclaimed their mounts, they would overtake them on the open country between here and the Palo Duro. One hopeless scenario after another plagued his thoughts as he leapt and skipped down the rugged path. Had any Comanche been alerted by the gunfire? He shook his head in anguish. The very thought of rescue by them was the height of desperation. Yet this deep into the Llano it was a practical one.

* * *

East of the Comancheria station, Texas Tonk showed Cole Hawker the lonely roadside grave dug by Renald for the slain stagecoach whip. Blood-tainted arrows lay in a pile beside it. Still detectable to the trained eye were signs the Comanche had done the killing, on cavalry mounts. Striking distance from the supposedly tame lodges of Indian Territory, the location was suggestive as well. The men rode on in silence, in time arriving at the scorched station site, where Texas led them to Beckert's corpse. By this time desert creatures had feasted on it. This was the final living horror from which Renald had saved Beckert by putting a bullet in his head. Beard and eyebrows survived to identify him. "Rest, trooper," remarked the big hide man from his saddle. That was all. He swung his horse around. A gust of wind delivered the telltale stench of rotting flesh, drawing them toward the fire-seared stagecoach. The men approached warily, riding abreast through scattered debris.

Hawk, smothering his nose in his cavalry neckerchief, turned toward his presumed man-eating companion. "Smells like dinner, eh?"

Texas stiffened. "One more joke, I eat *you*."

"Testy!" exclaimed the old horse soldier. Undaunted, he added, "Or ought I say, *tasty?*"

Before Texas could react, Hawk heeled his animal to the stage. A door still hung open, but gone was the scalped body that had splayed halfway out for Renald. Absent, too, was the belly-down corpse of the shotgun rider. Interpreting the confusion of prints and blood swaths on the ground, at least two bodies had been torn asunder and dragged away in pieces. Hawk peered into the stage's cabin and gasped. The open door had let the brush wolves in.

Like Renald before them, they left the dead where they lay in favor of gaining time. Twilight was imminent. Texas showed Hawk where the raiders had disappeared into North Scalp Gorge with Renald following, and sometime later, at dusk, he crowed with pride where his party had massacred the Comanche. Dismounted, he ripped a shattered arrow from the ground. "This mine," he said. "Next one for Renald."

"Just whatd'ya mean by that?" growled Hawk.

"I go with you," replied Texas, regaining his mount.

"You was instructed by Black Jack to deliver yer pay to Chief Buffalo Run and rendezvous with the column."

Texas tugged rein on his anxious pinto. "Maybe Buffalo Run chasing Renald."

Surprised, Hawk hauled back. He grasped the saddle horn in his meaty hands, pinning the reins. "You figure Buffalo Run would follow Renald into Comancheria?"

"Yes."

"Why didn't you save him the trouble when you had the chance?"

"I follow chief orders. Now I follow chief."

"What about following Davidson's orders? Yer an officer now."

"He got no eye out here."

"He don't? How ya figure me?" Hawk spit tobacco juice and thought it over. If he refused to take Texas along, he'd have to beat him silly. He sighed. "It's *yer* scalp, Corporal. First Comanche we encounter will carve it out. Till then, I reckon I could use yer skills."

Hawk was satisfied with the pace of their progress. The way from Fort Sill had been familiar and clear-cut, requiring no chin-scratching delays. By the light of the full moon they rode on, able to follow the pursuers' wide trail. He found himself aghast for Renald's sake at the number of unshod hoof marks overlaying Stardust's. The situation was perilous for everybody, but for Renald it was both less promising and more dangerous. Not only must he worry that some roaming Comanche band might attack before he could surrender Miss Little, but he had to fear fifteen or twenty Tonkawa dogging his heels too. The two men rode on, eyes scanning the prairie by night, stopping just once to rest themselves and their mounts.

The first foretelling of complications emerged at dawn when Texas spotted where four outriders had separated from the

Tonkawa party. That they had ridden fast ahead was obvious by the depth of their tracks where the ground was soft and by the gashes made where it was hard. From here Texas tracked the scouts while Hawk remained on the trail of the main body, heading due west. At last the scouts split into twos, perhaps to picket for Comanche ahead. Beyond, at the rim of the basin where Renald and Miss Little had camped, one pair had rendezvoused with the main body. Midway into the basin, Hawk and Texas, reunited, found the other pair.

Texas rolled one bloated body off the other.

Appraising the dead over Texas' shoulder, Cole Hawker shook his head in admiration of Scott Renald. "Friends of yers?"

The Indian righted himself, eyes aflame. "I bury 'em."

"I didn't bury *my* people," came the reply.

"I bury mine. You help me or you wait."

He tried to reason with Texas. "The longer we delay the more bodies you gonna find. Anytime Renald wants to cut their numbers he'll stake out a position with that Winchester of his. We can't overhaul him by burying every body we come across. And there'll be more." Gaining no reaction, he added, "Seems Buffalo Run didn't pause none to pay respects, neither."

Texas gestured toward one of the braves. "This my brother."

In an instant Hawk's risk increased. There'd be no controlling Texas if they found Renald alive. He considered drawing on the Indian and demanding his weapons but scratched his armpit instead. "Take yer time! But other braves'll die while you build yer brother's mound."

The Indian considered Hawk briefly with spent eyes. He crouched beside his brother's body. On what level ground existed in a dust-fill between boulders, he attempted to straighten the stiff limbs and cross one forearm over the chest. "This happen last night," he concluded.

No stranger himself to the signs of a decaying body, Hawk grunted agreement. He now saw a way to be rid of his dangerous companion. "Naturally, you'll want some time with yer brother … maybe take him home, sit over his body a few days."

"We very near. Only hours. *We ride.*" Texas sprinkled the corpse with a handful of earth while quietly chanting something.

When he finished, Hawk extended his tobacco stick to him. "Would offering up some of this help?"

Though for once Hawk had spoken to Texas with respect, even deference, the Indian reacted with a look of incredulity. He shook his head and grasped some earth for the second body. Then he sprang to his feet and returned to the waiting pinto. Hawk shrugged.

They had no difficulty following the trails, which led in a half circle around the basin and then up the steep and drafty dry wash. Welcoming them back to level ground was the scorching midday sun and a blast of heat. Unusual cloud formations for this season swept into the big, blue sky like veils of smoke. Hawk and Texas both recognized the lonesome butte known as Survivor's Bluff. Only there could riders find shade between here and the Palo Duro. If the Comanche had any scouts stationed on it, Laura Little might already be in their hands. Surveying the unforgiving country and the distance between points, Hawk wiped his brow. "That's some flatiron out there. We best let the horses blow 'fore they plum give out."

"You rest," answered Texas. "I ride."

Hawk shook his head. Just who was in charge here? He thrust his finger toward the rock. "If I was Renald, that's where I'd make my stand …" Turning back, he saw the Tonk's right eye contract and his nostril flare as if he was picking up a scent carried by the hot wind. Was he?

"Maybe they got lucky," added Hawk, unconvincingly. "Maybe they was smart and sat here till Renald lost patience. You can see where they squatted and ate their pemmican."

Texas dismissed Hawk's speculation with a click of the tongue. "They camp here because they ride with chief. He old. If chief not ride with them, was no need send my brother ahead." He heeled his horse forward onto the barren mesa. The white man sighed and followed, the corners of his mouth downturned under his beard. During the sweltering crossing, the two men uttered not a word to each other, though there were moments when Hawk was tempted to try. Pride prevented him—pride and the conviction that Texas was unreachable.

An hour later, with the butte looming high on the horizon, they caught sight of a blight on the landscape ahead. Drawing near on their suffering mounts, the spot became two, then four, then doubled again till it was clear they'd run into yet another spill of bodies—and more. Texas kicked his sweat-lacquered horse into a gallop, leaving Hawk in the rear yet again. Cursing, the bearded man heeled his mount, slowed by his abundance. One after another they drove their animals toward the site where Renald had dry-gulched his pursuers. From a distance they could see alarmed coyotes retreating to the sides and silhouetted birds rising aloft on vast wingspans.

Reaching the place, they reined their animals hard back, and Hawk held his neckerchief to his nose in revulsion. He'd not seen so many men down and destroyed since witnessing the ravages of cannon fire in the late war. Centripetal marks in the earth showed that fallen braves had dragged themselves toward a lone victim. Body parts lay scattered about, the scavengers having torn asunder the dead—and the dying too?—while fighting over sun-cooked meat. Weapons remained, a sign the Comanche hadn't done this, nor discovered it. Texas guided his mount through the carnage, followed by Hawk, who was glancing guardedly this way and that. At about the same instant both riders spotted the neck-up remains of Chief Buffalo Run in his feathered war bonnet.

Hawk remarked, "Least he was wearing his Sunday best."

Texas dove from the saddle, landing chest-first beside his chief's gnawed-off head. He clawed the bloodstained ground between head and torso and swore vengeance on the man responsible. Wailing, he spilled tears onto the parched, alkaline earth. Then he rose into a cross-legged position and swayed to and fro, his sobs leading him into a death chant. Hawk let him get it out. Each of the braves torn to pieces around their leader had been needed against the Comanche and Kiowa, and all had shared the promise of repopulating the tribe. With so many fighting men gone, the Tonkawa's very existence was threatened. For Texas, it was hard enough to find these remains on the desert floor; harder still, Hawk realized, to forfeit them to scavengers already full to bursting with the flesh of his people, friends.

Nudging his horse forward past the mourning Indian, he counted heads. "Eight deceased here, maybe more out there."

Behind him Texas muttered, "Enough got through."

Hawk studied the butte beyond. " 'Nuf to provide a trail of bodies." Then, "We're losing time, the time we gained riding fast."

Texas made a feverish lunge toward his horse and ripped his saddle gun from the slip. He was taking aim at the beasts pacing hungrily at the perimeter when Hawk raised a hand in protest. "You want the Comanche to hear? We got enough trouble with just one gun turned back at us! Besides, ain't wolves sacred to you?"

The Indian regarded his weapon with futility, frustration, before thrusting it back into the fringed buckskin. "I bury chief."

This time Hawk didn't protest. Groaning, he thumped down off his horse and unfastened his telescopic spade from the saddle pack. "It's gonna be one shallow grave!"

* * *

With Cole Hawker leaning on his tool, sweating from the work the men had completed in turns, Texas arranged the body parts in their resting place. According to custom, he pointed the feet west, and, bending a stiff, dismembered arm, laid a hand over the chest. Bandy-legged, he whirled a fistful of earth onto the remains, chanting a final prayer. Hawk began shoveling dirt into a burial mound.

Chapter Seven

Hawk and Texas interpreted the signs as a pair, the one mounted, the other on foot and leading his horse behind him. From the tracks heading west they read how Renald and Miss Little had ridden straight for the butte, whereas the remaining mounted Tonk, under fire, had split into two parties, each trying to gain it by angled approaches. The unshod tracks were the freshest. Observing the sheer wall of the rock, Hawk said, "No way to get a horse up there from this approach. Scott musta ridden around and found a way in. I figure he set the woman down someplace, then come over the top to take up that position. Yer friends clum up after him—under fire." He thrust his finger toward the butte. "See them horses under that ledge? There, to the right! Well, I ain't leaving *my* animal behind to go mountaineering."

"You take horses and follow Renald," said Texas. "I follow Tonkawa."

Hawk found himself smiling with amusement. "Corporal, I sure as hell don't take orders from you. And yer mission ain't to assassinate Renald. By climbing atop, yer going after him— not her."

"To get woman we must kill him. From start you think this."

Another thought struck Hawk. He frowned. "Yer friends find me leading yer empty mount, that'll be *my* end."

"Could be," the Indian replied.

"Texas, you plain agitate me. Plain."

Hawk scratched his beard. If Texas really intended to run afoul of the U.S. Army by exacting revenge upon Scott Renald, he surely hoped to redeem himself by returning with Miss Little. From here his thirst for blood would drive him to climb to Renald's most recent known position, but Renald would've fallen back to protect the woman, and Hawk might reach him first by following his original path. On balance, it was worth it to separate from Texas and ride alone. Besides, so long as he held Texas' horse there was a chance the vengeful injun could be brought under control in a pinch. He spit tobacco juice. "You win. I'll lead yer mount."

They rode to the base of the butte, where the abandoned horses had gathered. Matching some to the braves unaccounted for, Texas deduced which men had gone after Renald and Miss Little on foot. He alighted and held out the reins to his skeptical colleague.

Accepting them, Hawk asked, "Going after him with knife alone?"

"Rifle too heavy. Knife enough for Renald."

"Think you'll get that close? And what if you meet some Comanche?"

"If Comanche there, all us die."

Hawk gestured ahead. "You first …"

Texas gave him a halfhearted salute, which Hawk returned in equally careless fashion. Neither had much enthusiasm for the U.S. Cavalry but here they were in its employ. "Better take this …" added the white man, tossing him a canteen. "I got another couple o' full ones."

Texas spun off the cap and began gulping.

"Want a tin of something too?"

Texas handed back the canteen. "No time."

"Best take the time!" Belly spilling over his belt, Hawk began unbuckling a saddlebag, but Texas stopped him by turning his back and skipping toward the cliff wall.

* * *

Despite Renald's efforts to erase the signs of his expectoration, the pursuing Tonkawa found it, first by sniff, then by trained eye. Just a broken edge of crust remained. From there tracking him was easy. The path, first discerned by heel scrapes, led them due west across the butte, from stone to stone, each as hard and hot as the next, until they reached what sufficed as a traversable trail, imprinted with fresh, hurried boot prints. The sun was beginning to dip, the heat starting to lift, when they leaped as one onto a rock parapet and plunged their focus twenty feet to where a hatted figure was glimpsed ducking below a granite overhang and vanishing from view. Then all was still. Immediately the Tonkawa were on the move again. Descending cautiously, they noticed a shroud concealing the interior.

Far behind them, sweaty and dust-caked, Texas was lifting himself to the butte's rim when an echoing gunshot rattled the desert silence. He paused, chest heaving. Meantime, climbing Renald's horse path a distance away, Hawk heard it as well. He halted and scanned the rock formations ahead. Each man, on his own side of the butte, instinctively awaited a second shot.

It followed. At once Texas started down the trail of boot marks and blood spatter while Hawk kicked his mare hard in the ribs, one hand grasping the pinto's reins.

* * *

Renald lowered his canteen and peered around the blanket he'd hung over the cave opening from the inside. With each gunshot another bright hole had appeared in it. "I make out four … no, five Tonk," he said between heaving breaths. "At least one more could be searching for our animals." He wiped his brow in the joint of his arm, coating the sleeve. Opposite him, Miss Little had backed herself into the cave wall, clutching her weapon, the blue shawl bracketing her face. Beams of light cast by the perforated wool cut between her and him, dust particles rising within.

"Still so many braves?" Her voice trembled. "What happened out there? All that shooting …"

Satisfied the Tonkawa weren't fool enough to storm the cave just yet, Renald propped the rifle against the wall and buried his face in his hands. He sank to the floor, features hidden. After about a minute he lowered his hands and put the blame on her. "I lost track how many people've died because of you. And those out there'll die too … allies of the United States Army."

Almost inaudibly, she replied, "You don't see me crying."

He glared up at her. "No, ma'am, I don't. But then—to you—the only good Tonk is a dead Tonk."

She shrugged in the gloom of the cavern. "Should I feel otherwise?"

"You might," he said. "It's those people who lead the U.S. Cavalry and its agents to rescue more grateful women than you. Got me all twisted inside, killing Tonk to benefit Comanche. I'm on the wrong side of everybody but the Comanche."

On the prairie south of the Tonk Forest where he'd pledged to help, Renald could not have foreseen he would become so invested in her struggle, that it would cost more lives, that he would take any, let alone so many. He shook his head, wondering why he hadn't tried to negotiate a truce when he had them pinned down. Had he unconsciously made the Tonkawa suffer for what the Comanche had done to him? He didn't pose this question to himself just yet. Back at the post, "Johnny Reb Renald" was despised by some, white and black, for another choice he'd made to fight. If he was lucky and got back, he would face Tonk scouts as disdainful of him as the black soldiers were. This he pondered under Miss Little's gaze.

She stepped forward and gestured with the pistol. "If we break out firing, you think we can make our mounts?"

Renald frowned with annoyance. "Holster it," he replied, "and stop thinking."

A third shot rang out. Another streak of light appeared through a fresh hole in the blanket, further illuminating their confines. The peal of a ricocheting bullet rang around them. They met flat on the floor, covering their heads. When Renald rose, rubbing the sound out of his ear, he saw fear in her alert, green eyes. He continued, "Trying to shoot our way out is just what they want us to do. Longer they wait, the greater the chance your people will show. Comanche-moon raiding parties should be returning about now. You best believe somebody heard that gunfire this morning. Those Tonk are figuring the same."

"Perhaps they will save themselves, go home," she said.

"Nobody's going home reward-less who's left his chief on the battlefield. Sundown'll raise their courage."

A look of alarm softened into one of relief. "You think we have till then?"

"Only way makes sense for them." Abruptly, he added, "Let's eat."

"I beg your pardon?"

"You oughta be hungry … Beans?"

"Surely you're teasing, Mr. Renald. This is no time."

"On the contrary, ma'am."

Ducking his head, he swung to her side and lowered himself to the items waiting beside her mat. With one hand he grabbed a tin of beans, with the other a one-talon opener. He ground the lid awry and bent it back.

She crossed her arms. "No thanks."

"Suit yourself." He took her fork and dug in.

"I'm supposed to watch you eat while hungry Tonk lick their lips outside?"

"They ain't pushing in for a while yet," he replied between chews. "Meantime, these are good beans …" He jiggled the can.

She shook her head.

"In that case, can't hurt to keep an eye out …"

She peeled her gaze from him and stepped across the space, passing treacherously through the beams of light. Next to the leaning Winchester she gained a sideways posture protected by the angle of the cave. With trembling fingers she created a gap between wool and rock.

"Easy does it …" he cautioned. "They think it's me, they'll shoot your nose clean off."

She blinked away the glare. "I don't see anybody …"

"You will."

"There's a muzzle sticking up behind a rock, pointing skyward ..."

"They're pretending otherwise. But they're watching."

His meal down, Renald relaxed his right leg and reached deep into his pocket. He withdrew the two boxes of ammunition and emptied them in a pile, casting the cartons away. Rising, he extended his hand to her. "Your scarf," he demanded. "Pass it here."

She hesitated. "Why mine?"

"Because I'm asking for *yours*." He flapped his fingers.

Eying him suspiciously, she untied and surrendered the garment. He balled the fabric and used it to wipe the can clean.

She crinkled her nose. "This time, spare me the promise of washing it."

He withdrew the Indian dagger strapped to his chest. "Easy to pop these casings, just get the blade in here." Demonstrating with a single shell, he dislodged the bullet from the inch-long copper casing, then emptied the gunpowder into the canister. "See?"

She laughed, bitterly. "You intend to throw that at them?"

"No, Miss Little," he replied, "I intend to send up a black cloud. In the late war, we used to make these from pieces of coal stuffed with gunpowder, called 'em torpedoes. Sabotaged Yankee steam engines by slipping 'em into the firebox supply." He planted his hands on his thighs and got to his feet, then pulled off the knife strap and dusted his hands on his hips. "You got forty-nine more to go. Should be good for the three ounces we need. Twenty minutes work while I keep watch."

"That's a lot of ammunition to use on the chance somebody'll see."

"If instead we wait for the Tonk to attack, tonight they'll tear down this cover and bust in here. We'll get off five, maybe six rounds. Two or three braves will fall before they overpower us. They'll make you watch while I'm divvied up for chow-chow, limb by limb."

They exchanged positions and she followed his example. For a while they were both silent. Renald held his eye on the confirmed five Tonk outside, closer in than before but hanging their heads low. One kept his rifle barrel trained on the cave entrance while the others powwowed. When Renald finally got a clear shot at a protruding head he squeezed off a round. It sprayed some dust and the target ducked. The brave with the rifle returned fire, piercing the blanket and making yet another glinting hole. Renald fired back but missed again.

Miss Little was regarding him with alarm. "Must you pick the fight?"

"Just signaling we're still in the contest," Renald explained.

A heated discussion was underway outside. From behind the broken rock shielding them, the braves had to raise their voices to hear each other. Renald caught enough of it. "Exactly," he said.

Miss Little spoke. "Exactly what?"

"They're debating what to do. One buck has the idea of setting fire to this sheet with a flaming arrow. Another warns of the smoke. They'll sit tight and wait for sundown. How's it coming?"

"Making progress," she said, her voice strained as she tried another cartridge, "but some of these are tough to pry open."

"Careful. We don't want that blade slipping and cutting you."

Eyeing him, she continued her work. Minutes passed. The cavern chimed with the sounds of cartridges chipped apart and casings discarded.

On guard for movement outside, Renald resisted the urge to make conversation. Sharing leads to more sharing. Like all plains officers, he preferred the hush of the ride to chitchat. For a woman, Miss Little was not much of a talker herself, fortunately. And yet, he acknowledged, there was much that might be said between them. Throughout this journey he'd found himself increasingly inclined to talk to her, and to listen when she spoke. He drew a long breath and, fatefully, broke the silence.

"I knew your husband's father, Chief Iron Mountain," he said. "Fact, I dealt with him till he ended the captive trade."

This was his first reference to Talking Moon as her spouse. Till now he'd avoided it. But their mission was about family, and it was time he accepted she had a husband, not just a son, even though he was a red man. "Some of those women held for trade were in real bad shape," he added.

Miss Little glanced up from her piles of powder and copper. "Surely you did save some of them. Some had difficulties."

"That's speaking mild."

"I tried to help. I did help. Conversing in English was a balm. But to a grown woman, there's no new way."

"Except by force," he said. "They were broken in like feral horses, tamed to a savage way."

She restrained tears. "I suffered as well."

"*You,* ma'am?" By her reaction, he realized she was equating the plight of captives with her return to Fort Worth. "Hardly," he scoffed.

She interrupted her work to expose the scarred underside of her left wrist.

He was unsurprised. "I saw those ruts two days back. Didn't want to give you cause to try it again. So here we are." If she'd hoped for sympathy, it wasn't coming from him.

She dried her eyes. "You can be a hard man, Scott."

"Wherever the Quahada followed the buffalo," he continued, "I followed them when women and girls went missing. But in Iron Mountain's camp, I never once laid eyes on you."

Patting her eyes with her sleeve, she responded. "I wasn't for trade."

"You sure weren't. But you might've glimpsed me once or twice."

"I was hidden away when white men came to camp. I'm sure you never saw my husband, either."

"Till Iron Mountain died, his son was just another brave to us. We knew he had one, though—a strong one. What makes you so sure we never met? Maybe he sat at his father's side."

She shook her head. "Not during talks with you—or any white man. Iron Mountain avoided that."

"Avoided it?" Renald was impatient. "Keep talking ..."

"You'd have seen he wasn't full red."

He blinked. "Talking Moon ... a half blood?"

She nodded. "It doesn't show unless you get close."

"Those of us got close got scalped," he replied.

Breaking into another cartridge, she continued, "He's as dark as the others—but his eyes are blue, like yours."

Rifle in hand, Renald strode across the gap between them. "All those years Iron Mountain kept a captive wife ... and we never knew?"

"Wouldn't you have sounded charge if you did? She looked after me during my betrothal. I had someone to speak English with. In fact, she'd been a schoolteacher."

"A *schoolteacher*?" Renald stood at the edge of a precipice. Gathering himself for the question to follow, he drew a fortifying breath. "Remember her name?"

She lifted her chin and answered serenely, "She was called Ma Kahpenakwu Mia—She Rode West."

"Not her *Comanche* name, damn it. Her white name!"

She swallowed. "Her name was Margaret."

To an observer, after a brief show of exhilaration, his face might've registered disappointment, even loss. He bent his knee to the cave floor and asked, "Ever learn her surname?"

"If she once properly introduced herself, it was when I couldn't listen."

He understood. "Is she alive?"

Miss Little shook her head. "She returned to the Great Spirit. Before Iron Mountain did."

He rested his forearm on his thigh and dragged his forlorn gaze across the dusty ground. Disappointed though he was, he was very much alarmed too.

"Scott?"

He should tell her. He must tell her. But not now. First he had to get them out of here. No distractions.

"Scott?" she repeated, cocking her head. "Were you aware of a woman named Margaret who went missing?"

He hesitated, then unbuttoned his chest pocket and withdrew a money clip thick with photographs. He selected a battered portrait of a woman in her wedding gown. With a neutral expression, he passed it to her. She examined it, stunned.

"You only knew her squawified," he said.

"But it's her. Without a doubt."

"She was on our rescue list a long spell. But I never gave up looking."

Returning the picture, she offered, "She came to love Iron Mountain. And of course she cherished her son. No rescued captive would've betrayed her."

"With Margaret his mother and Iron Mountain his father," he ventured, "Talking Moon must be real handsome."

"So is our son," she responded, longingly. "He has his father's eyes. He's a smart boy, speaks better English than his father. I was teaching him to read and write—it will be important to the tribe one day."

"Three-fourths white," he reflected, shaking his head in disbelief. "To my mind he's one of us—in moccasins."

"His skin is white, but his spirit is red. Nothing can change that."

"Your spirit was changed over time, wasn't it? You could give the boy a chance." He slipped the wad of pictures back into his pocket, rising. "Sounds like it was best for everybody I didn't find her."

He turned his back, resting the rifle barrel on his shoulder and drumming the magazine. She detected his unease, his sudden remove. "You and Margaret would be close in age ..."

"We were at that," he muttered, peering out the sheet, indifferent to the danger.

"The Margaret I knew left a husband behind."

"Same with the Margaret I looked to find."

"Our first morning together, you said something about unsolved loss being the worst kind ..."

"Yes, ma'am, I did. The grief never stops."

"But was it you, Scott? Were you that man?"

He stepped before her, a darkened presence. "No, ma'am. Her husband was a homesteader name of Chase."

"I see," she said. "Silly me ..."

"Twenty-odd years back," he said, "Comanche raided the Chase spread near Camp Worth, started a fire that ripped through the place. One of the women's bodies was burnt so bad we couldn't identify her. Another woman was taken. Who died, and who was taken was a mystery—until now."

"Now that you know it was Margaret who was taken," she said softly, "who was the one who died?"

He replied, "Now I know it was my wife."

At first she stared into his shadowy eyes. Then, under the weight of his gaze, she looked away—with a feeling of shame? He felt a pulled-back, deadened sensation. It was her band of Comanche that did it, the people she was running back to with his help. The cold moment passed. At last he knew.

Mustering the courage, she conveyed her sadness. "So sorry for you, for her. I did notice the ring you wear. You told me you haven't any children ..."

"She was with child, Laura. Would've been our first."

A hush. Then, delicately, "Forgive me raising the unhappy memories, Scott. There can't be any worse."

"It's easier your knowing."

He began to revive, to value the sharing. Serving his life on a skillet was uncomfortable, but for a very long time he hadn't had a woman to share with. His eyes rested on her in a new and penetrating way. "Fact is, you resemble her. In body and spirit. Your yellow hair. The way you hold your chin up when you think you're right and drop it when you know you're wrong. Time I lost her, she was a young lady too."

She was quiet. Then, "Is that why you decided to help me? Because I remind you of her?"

"Maybe. But there's the boy. I was thinking of him as well. You reckon Talking Moon could be talked into surrender?"

"Only in defeat. If he lives, we might live on the reservation together."

"Together? On the reserve? Come to your senses. Your family would lock you up first."

"No," she replied. "They would lock me up *again*."

"Find yourself a Christian husband," he said, "and they'll have no say any more about your competence."

"One husband at a time, Scott."

She dropped the last shell into the pile of empties and extended the knife to him, handle first. "Ready!" she said.

"Good. Let's see if we can't stick this lid shut." He found a jerky stick at the bedside and, lowering himself, rolled it between his palms till it softened. Next, he gummed it around the can's rim and pushed down the lid. It stuck.

"Unlikely to hold," she observed. "But what were you saying about a scarf having many uses in the desert?" She reached toward his collar, hooked a finger through the center loop of his neckerchief, and slowly pulled the knot apart and the fabric to her. Offering him a crafty look, she wrapped it tightly around the tin, securing it with a top knot. "Now we've got our torpedo—dressed in cavalry yellow."

"Fair enough, Laura," he replied, "and fitting."

Part III
Dead Meat

Chapter Eight

Renald extended the Winchester stock first. "You say you're a good shot. Alert your people."

Laura Little half smiled.

She got into place on the far side of the shroud while he crouched down and gathered a fistful of wool in his left hand. He edged the blanket up enough to create an outlet for the explosive in his other hand. After a nod from him she inched the rifle barrel into daylight, a movement detectable to anybody on the lookout. The Tonkawa were hardly dozing. A gunshot sounded, breaking the desert silence that had prevailed for many minutes. Where her steel muzzle glinted in the sunlight, chips of stone flew. She jerked back and flattened herself against the cave wall, gripping the rifle upright. Eyes aflame with fear and expectation, she observed Renald on one knee beside the blanket. He tested the canister's weight in his grasp. "Here goes ..."

With a swing of his arm he rolled it outside, the vigorous clattering of tin on stone an eerie overture. A second shot rang out. A fourth sunbeam appeared through the blanket. Across the way, the brave was jacking his finger lever for a third shot when another warrior slapped the barrel down. Cursing each other, they grappled over the gun, rising as one into the open air.

Laura Little leveled her weapon again.

Though the tussling braves made easy targets, she dedicated her attention to the slowing roll of the can. It stopped just paces from them, and she took her shot.

A blast of noise and light followed. Riddled by shrapnel and blackened from gunsmoke, both warriors fell dead onto the rocks behind. A dark billow issued from charred limestone bedrock.

Miss Little pulled back. "Two more!"

Renald turned down his lips, letting go the shroud. "Ain't becoming to take pleasure in it."

He motioned for the return of his rifle. Unhesitatingly, she tossed it across the space between them.

"Get back," he cautioned, then parted the cloth and fired two random shots. The rounds glanced off boulders shielding their besiegers, but the message registered—*stay put*. He could afford no more of such shots.

Shouting, the surviving Tonk berated each other. Those out front seemed to be communicating with others off to the sides, maybe four in all. If the exchange of gunfire and signal cloud had coalesced the enemy, it wasn't a setback for Renald and Miss Little. The Tonk were again concentrated in one place, and with that black beacon scaling the horizon their timetable had accelerated. If they didn't withdraw to their horses soon and hightail it back, they'd never see their women and children again. In their heated exchanges, Renald could sense growing desperation.

* * *

The explosion echoed far and wide over the rough terrain. Texas and Hawk both saw the smoke ball ascend like a piece of coal toward the sun, visible at five miles, then ten, and then others saw it too. The Indian halted his feverish pursuit, catching his breath, his eyes following the expanding puff into the blue sky. Then, with renewed vigor, he resumed his advance down Renald's unmistakable trail, kicking up dust.

Meantime, the smoke told Hawk where to diverge from the horse path he was climbing. With a screak of leather he twisted in his saddle to look for anything resembling a clear way uphill, or at least a traversable area. He dismounted and led his animals across a boulder slide. Rounding a stone wall, they were stopped by a bed of impenetrable cholla. He yanked his lead horse around, cursing. Other attempts, one thornier or steeper than the next, also failed to link to anything. Ultimately, sweating through his shirt, he accepted that he must return to the original trail. On the step-by-step descent, he continued searching the landscape for an alternative and at last noticed a dry wash off to the right. Snaking between sandstone outcrops, it seemed wide enough—but would it lead anywhere? Between here and there was a bed of stiff sideoats grama. Hawk made slow progress through it. To avoid unseen hoof traps, he cautiously tested the way with his boot while holding tight the lead horse's reins. Sensing his insecurity, the mare shook her bridle and halted in protest more than once. This time, however, Hawk was on the right track. In minutes the run-off trail delivered them to the summit.

With cool late-afternoon gusts whipping at his body, he clambered onto even ground and beheld the bleak plateau of Survivor's Bluff. Before him, jagged saw-toothed formations stood erect, casting long, easterly shadows. He stepped forward, sharpening his senses, his free hand finding the butt of his six-shot.

Here Cole Hawker felt more vulnerable than he had on the desert floor. A Tonk brave concealed behind any of these rocks could pose a greater danger than a party of ten in open country. Not only was Texas absent to protect him from his fellow tribesmen, but Hawk was suspiciously leading the Indian's pony—a sure inducement to ambush. He even considered the possibility that Texas himself was hiding with his blade. At any moment Hawk might feel flint rip through his flesh. He braced for attack, feeling a tingle at the base of his skull, his tangled beard moistening with sweat. For twenty cautious paces he swept his eyes from side to side, registering nothing but the threatening monotony of the terrain. When his horse suddenly snorted and bobbed her head, he tugged her reins in alarm and halted both animals. The wind howled while he listened for a reaction. Nothing. He advanced. A dozen paces on they came to the edge of a rugged natural arena. Rather than being able to reach out and touch the nearest rock, the closest formations were a stone's throw ahead, on the opposite rim. Lowering his gaze, he glimpsed fighting men staked out below. He eased back.

The expert hunter and veteran of three wars considered which rifle to arm himself with—his long-barreled, high-caliber Sharps buffalo rifle or Texas' old Henry, booted now on his horse. With the 34-inch and .52-caliber Sharps, Hawk could accurately deliver the most powerful rifle shot in the world, but its single-shot loading mechanism would limit him to about ten rounds per minute. As for the repeater, it was a comfortable gun in his hands. He'd carried one in the service, bought with his own money. But was Texas' gun reliable? Its manufacturer had long ago replaced it with the Winchester. Grunting, he pulled the heavy Sharps from its slip. He could use it to blast stone, giving one cartridge the force of many.

His survival depended on knowing the exact number of men below and their placement. At risk of detection he must complete a comprehensive visual sweep. He crawled forward and edged his nose out. Seen from the back, two braves had concealed themselves behind a parapet opposite an opening in the stone shrouded by fabric. The sun glinted off their silky hair, which fell in bands over their shoulders. To their right a pair of bodies lay in the area blackened by the explosion. Above the cavern on a thin shelf squatted a rifle-wielding warrior. Further to the left on the opposite rim was a sixth man guarding two mounts, one of them recognizable as Renald's flaxen sorrel. Forming the backdrop was the butte's irregular northern perimeter, the color of pie crust, and beyond it the yellows and reds of the mesa blanketed by a tranquil, pale sky.

The brave opposite him on the ledge raised his chin, and Hawk withdrew in haste. As he ducked down, expecting gunfire, he thought he saw something animated on the floor of the desert beyond—something moving fast. It warranted another look, despite the danger.

He pushed his nose out again.

A rifle shot sounded, followed closely by the *ching* of a glancing bullet.

Stone shavings peppered his face. Wiping them away, he streaked blood on his cheek. Hawk had given away his position but in doing so confirmed a patch rolling over the plains. If not for the clear sky, he might've confused it for the racing shadow of a small cloud. In a southerly motion it was fast approaching the base of the butte. Distracted as they were by the explosion and its aftermath, the Tonk did not see them coming.

"Comanche," he muttered.

To Hawk they were a welcome sight. He imagined what was likeliest to follow. The Tonkawa would fight and die, the woman would ride on with the Comanche, and he'd ride back with Renald his prisoner. That would be plenty gratifying, and success enough. He grinned. The cavalry would continue the search for Laura Little in just days. For now, he needed to keep the Tonk contained. Clutching his fifteen-pound Sharps, he got behind a boulder to his right. He must demonstrate his firepower. The stone entirely shielded him from another attack while affording an unimpeded view eastward. At that instant he happened to spot Texas emerging from the terrain about a hundred feet away, straining for breath, squinting into the sun, trying to make sense of what *he* saw: above the cave, a bent-knee brave was taking aim at a target opposite; scattered others below and beyond were observing the action. Uncertain, the brave was shifting his barrel left and right.

Hawk could see Texas turning his way as he traced the line of fire. When their eyes met, the Indian straightened up in shock. Hawk merely greeted him with a half-hearted salute before pivoting around the boulder and returning fire. For an average marksman it would have been a lucky shot.

* * *

Within their sanctuary, Renald and Miss Little heard the thunderous boom and felt their stone confines shudder as blasts of dust issued from above and rubble rained down beyond the woolen blanket. Something heavy thudded to the ground out there, propelling a dust-roll under the fringe. Gagging in the billow, Renald took Miss Little by the hand and led her deeper into the cavern. The circulating dust blotted out the light.

"Is this the end?" she sobbed in his arms.

"It sure is for that buck fell out there," he said between coughs. "That was a buffalo rifle's discharge." Clearing his throat, he added, "I reckon I know who fired it too."

Then they heard a big, raspy voice cry, "Texas! Tell 'em to stand down. You don't, you'll be the last Tonkaway riding the Llano."

In response, another voice—in the native tongue—yelled entreaties. Protests from the others followed.

Miss Little remained in Renald's embrace. In her ear, he whispered, "That's Cole Hawker, a hide man and retired horse soldier. He's got 'em pinned down but they won't surrender. Texas Tonk was one of 'em that took you. He scouts for the army."

She shivered in his hold. "You think they're riding point?" she asked.

"Don't sound so alarmed—that would be plum perfect."

"But if the army gets hold of you ... didn't you say you could face prosecution?"

"The safety of a guardhouse cell seems mighty fine just now," he answered.

Light was again making its way through the roused dust and into the chamber.

"Scott!" Hawk cried out. "You okay in there?"

Lest he yell back in her ear, Renald separated himself and followed the strengthening beams of light to the opening. "The woman is okay too, Hawk!"

"Let me hear her say it, Scott. I come a long way fer that!"

Renald motioned to her. "Well, tell him."

She hesitated.

"Get your head screwed on straight, Laura. The man's risking his life for you."

After a false start, she called out, "I'm Laura Little and I'm unharmed."

Satisfied, Hawk answered, "That was some signal you managed to send up, Scott! In no time this place will be swarming with Comanche."

"That's the idea!" Renald yelled back. "You commissioned?"

"I got a note here addressed to you—from Black Jack Davidson." Then, "Texas, yer people don't throw down them weapons I'm gonna discharge this one again."

"Maybe I go for gun myself!" the Indian responded. "Two rifles alone there."

Laura Little and Renald exchanged looks. He read renewed fear in her face.

* * *

From behind his weapon, Hawk replied, "Be my guest, injun! Make your move."

Texas made none.

The last thing Hawk needed was for Texas to get behind him with that knife. Hastily he formed a plan. "If you wanna get outta this alive and regain yer horse, best remember yer a corporal in the United States Army. Sitting in yer pocket is three months' fair wages. Yer people oughta get it, and get their bucks safe back too!"

He could see Texas' chest rise and fall as he mulled what to do. In a moment the fickle tracker cupped his hands around his mouth and began translating Hawk's words to his fellow fighting men. They shouted back scornfully.

Hawk understood. "Corporal, I'm killing my voice shouting. If you still ride with the U.S. Cavalry, let's talk this through!"

The Indian stood stock-still for a long moment, gripping the waist of his service pants. He glanced from Hawk to his people, then back again. Finally, he thrust a heel against the ground in frustration and then started making his way to the hunter's position while the braves hurled abuse at him. Scrambling from stone to stone, once or twice he disappeared from view. "I lose sight of you ..." the big man cautioned, "... I start blasting your brothers!" Unnoticed by Texas, he leaned the Sharps in front of him, freeing both hands. From his jacket he withdrew the sealed communication from Lieutenant Colonel Davidson to Renald. He ripped it open and scanned the chicken scratch. In the text, Davidson predictably appealed to Renald's loyalty, demanding that he and Hawk deliver Laura Little to Fort Sill or to any troop encountered en route. *Your commission,* he wrote, *to trade for hostages and carry out reconnaissance is hereby terminated. Following Miss Little's safe return, you shall present yourself to me, whether I be behind my desk or in the field, to write your report.*

Just as Hawk was reaching the end of the order, Texas raised himself to the hide man's position, tunic and pants sweat-sodden and dust-caked. Though his eyes were white hot, he appeared spent, as much from anguish as from exhaustion.

"That's close enough," Hawk warned, restoring the sheet to its envelope. He lowered his gun hand.

"What you think I do?" Texas responded, heaving for breath. "Kill you?"

"Choose this moment to try, I'd sure enjoy the advantage. Yer done worn out. Next time ride yer horse."

"You right about that," muttered Texas, hands on knees. "You here first."

"Yer a tracker. I'm a hunter. Now drink."

Hawk swung him a canteen. The Indian heaved it high in the air and sucked it like a starved calf.

"Hey, easy on that!"

Texas thrust it back, and Hawk said, "Look, a stalemate down there means yer friends are dead—and so are you." He added, "I seen Comanche approaching ..."

Texas stepped forward. "Comanche? Where?"

"Yonder." Hawk pointed with a nod of his whiskers. "By now they must be at the foot of the rock. No telling how fast they find us."

"Give me rifle," Texas demanded, voice rising.

Cole Hawker shook his head.

Cupping his hands around his mouth, Texas moved in the direction of his tribesmen.

Hawk drew his short gun. "Shut yer mouth, Texas."

Texas dropped his hands to his sides, startled. Hawk was surprisingly fast.

"If they rush the cave I gotta kill 'em," said Hawk, "after I kill you."

"So what you want?"

Hawk whispered, "I got us a plan to save everybody."

"Us? What plan?"

"First yer friends lay down them weapons, then Renald and the woman come out."

The Indian's eyebrows strained to meet. "Tonkawa no way disarm in Comancheria."

"They will if you convince 'em. Renald'll face justice back at Sill. That's punishment, ain't it?"

Texas scowled.

"Face it, Corporal—should the Comanche overtake us, we need him. We can all skedaddle back to them ponies they left and ride out before it's too late."

"We not ride with Renald he carry weapon," said Texas.

Hawk holstered his revolver. "In this here situation everybody ought forget his pride. We need Renald's gun against the Comanche."

"But he not loyal."

Hawk shook Davidson's order in his knobby fist. "Our duty is to give him the choice."

"What happen to weapons Tonkawa throw down?"

He pondered it. "They travel alongside me on Renald's mule. Don't you fret, Texas. Should the Comanche overhaul us, you'll get 'em back—fast."

Texas scoffed. "White man's promise …"

"You got a better plan to get Renald outta that cave and save yer scalps?" When Texas offered none, Hawk continued. "Good. See that mule down there? Load it up with every gun, bow, and blade. Next, serve Renald this letter. He'll come out."

"I want my mount first. Then I try."

"You get yer mount back when you deliver Renald and the woman to me."

Texas rolled his shoulders, making them crack. "Maybe I kill Renald in there."

Hawk gathered strands of his sooty beard in his hand. Texas killing Renald would simplify everything. But the Indian was no match for him.

"He kill my brother," Texas reminded.

"Way it looked, yer brother jumped him! Yet Renald bested two fighting men with surprise on their side. I trust you'll fare better straight up against him, panting like a dog." Hawk extended his free hand. "Surrender that blade and do as I tell you."

The Indian tracker's chest rose and fell within his filthy tunic. Then in a lightning movement he took possession of the envelope.

Maybe Texas had some fight left in him after all. Hawk avoided a confrontation over the knife. "Don't say nothing to nobody about the Comanche near," he cautioned. "Think it through, or it'll be the end of you Tonkaway."

"Comanche here make difference," Texas responded, cryptically. Swinging around, he commenced a cautious descent, the handle of his blade protruding from the scabbard strapped across his back. Hawk wondered if he could—would—take Renald.

Chapter Nine

Texas reached the bottom. Rather than going for the mule, as ordered, he simply made a beeline for the cave. "I'll be damned," Hawk groaned, shaking his head in contempt of himself. He might've predicted Texas would use the letter as a pretext to get near Renald, disregarding the rest. He reached for the gun best suited to the likeliest of outcomes and began prioritizing his targets.

"Real bad day for the Tonk," he muttered.

* * *

From his vantage point behind the shroud, Renald kept a wary eye on Texas. "Stay back," he told Miss Little.

Holding aloft the envelope, Texas avoided the glares of his reproachful tribesmen and stopped short of the shrouded opening. At his feet was the body of the warrior brought down by Hawk. The corpse lay lengthwise, face flattened against the ground. A rifle lay orphaned beside it. Texas rolled the body over with his boot. It settled. He chanted a prayer that started:

He ya he yo, ya he e
He ya he yo, ya he e
He ya he yo, ya he e

Behind him, his tribesmen chimed in with yelps and whoops and repetitions. Renald listened for threatening sounds or phrases but heard nothing of ill intent. It was not a scalp song. Nevertheless, he evaluated Texas as an opponent. Frankly, he looked in no condition to fight, if that was his intention. The powerful arms that had pulled him to these heights hung slack with fatigue, his head sagged between hunched shoulders, and his eyes blinked in craters inky from sleeplessness. Yet this was still a man driven by blood-right. The trail of bodies he'd followed—those of his own people—ended here, at a dead Tonk doormat. No matter that Renald had exercised a rearguard defense, his original deception had sparked the chase in which the Tonkawa had lost their chief and best warriors. Surely in Texas' mind only one man could be blamed.

Renald brought up the Winchester just as Texas reached for the rifle.

But Hawk was faster than either of them. A shot plunged into the earth at Texas' feet, chipping stone and halting his movement. "Don't make me do you with yer own gun!"

To avoid blinking, Renald viewed Texas through his eyelashes. Suddenly the Indian passed from sight behind the blanket. Next, a hand appeared parting the cloth, and he stepped into the chilled interior. Renald leveled the barrel of his rifle.

"Hello again," he said.

Texas' eyes fell upon the Tonkawa knife strapped across Renald's chest. He gathered himself with visible effort, sneering, "I should kill you."

"You sure got cause—but we were running, and they were chasing."

Texas saw Laura Little lingering a few steps back of Renald. "You come long way," he told her, "in wrong direction."

Before she could respond, Renald told her to stay out of it. He nodded toward the envelope in Texas' grasp. "That for me?" He received it, noting its torn edges. "I recall you don't read, Texas. So Hawk's reminded himself what's expected. That's good. Many ways a man can turn out here. Take yourself ... you're turning this way and that."

Texas did not reply, his dark form fringed by the light piercing the blanket behind.

Bracing the stock of his rifle against his hip, Renald kept his weapon ready as he freed a hand. "Unfold it and pass it here," he said.

Texas complied. Reaching behind his right shoulder, he let light into the chamber to read by.

Renald flashed him a critical eye. "Texas, I'm aware of that blade you're carrying, and the nearness of your hand to it. Count the number of movements you need. All I gotta do is pull this trigger."

With that, Renald delved into the order.

"What does it say?" Laura Little demanded.

Watching him digest it, Texas spoke: "You come with me, you not die. Ride to Sill. To Davidson, I accuse you."

"That's the way to do it," replied Renald, meeting Texas' gloomy eyes again.

Laura Little stepped out of the darkness. *What does it say?*

Renald turned to her with a sigh. "Laura, I'll fight the Tonkawa to save my skin and maybe yours too, but not the U.S. Cavalry. Don't you see?"

149

As he was stuffing the letter into his hip pocket, she drew her pistol and shot Texas in the chest. Renald bent his knees at the sound of her gunfire. He saw the Indian fall backward with a look of astonishment, tearing down the blanket. Texas landed on his back outside in a swell of dust, heels coming to rest on the ribs of the warrior who'd fallen before him. There was no sign he'd reached for his blade.

Light flooded the chamber as Renald slid Laura Little a scowl. "That's the Comanche in you! I shoulda known!"

Gunfire erupted outside, the booming report of Hawk's buffalo rifle thundering over the rest. The walls around them trembled.

Together, guns aimed at the opening, Renald and Miss Little stepped deeper within as the gunfight raged without. In seconds a lanky, bare-shouldered figure stumbled into the frame, swinging a rifle barrel toward them. Shoulder to shoulder each got off a round as another shot roared from outside, jerking the long-haired silhouette. Bloodied front and back, the warrior added height to the pile of corpses at their doorstep.

A hush ensued, at last broken by Hawk's booming voice: "Coming down, Scott!"

Hoof thunder followed.

Now, with a sideways motion of his rifle, Renald butted the pistol from Laura Little's hand. She moved for it, but he pushed her down and collected it himself.

Securing the weapon against the small of his back, he said, "If you fill Hawk with lead, I'll hang too." He shook his head in disgust. "What'd you do that for?"

Disarmed and admonished, she froze, speechless, her expression blank.

A scruffy mass filled the wall of light. With a boot planted on the mound of bodies as if they were dead game and the Henry's barrel resting on his shoulder, Cole Hawker called inside, "Everybody all right in there?"

"Coming out," Renald grumbled.

Ducking under the granite overhang, they emerged, dusty and squinting below their hat brims. Renald gripped Laura Little by the elbow.

Hawk made way for her, his gaze plunging. The drawstring having slipped out somewhere, her tattered blouse exposed the arcs of her breasts to a tall man. "A-la-bama!" he exclaimed. "If it ain't our fair Comanche squaw," he added—to her frown.

The men traded nods of acknowledgement.

"Been time," said former captain to ex-sergeant.

"A spell," replied Hawk, his jawline bulging from a wad of chaw.

Hawk and Renald had served in different regiments but were acquainted from civilian encounters at trading and army posts across Indian Territory and north Texas. Hawk was too coarse for Renald to like much. In fact, Renald had once seen him slide a drunken challenger clear down a saloon bar by the neck, the patrons making way, till he knocked his victim cold on the piano box.

The big man could've used a saloon right now. "I believe I've earned a drink if you've got one."

Renald shook his head. "Wish I could reward you with one. You're bleeding, Hawk."

Hawk touched his wounded cheek. "Got off easy with this." Then, to her, "Yer welcome, ma'am."

"For what?" she fired back.

"Saving you from them bucks is all."

"I've got Scott to thank for that."

"Well, you ain't the first woman failed to acknowledge my efforts. I'm done hurt." To Renald, he said, "That was *some* shooting you did from that ridge. Might get into the history books as the Survivor's Bluff Massacre."

Renald winced. "We're burning daylight. Did they find my animals?"

"Lookee there." Hawk pointed over Renald's shoulder, adding, "Couldn't paint it prettier." Atop a boulder-strewn path, mule and sorrel were silhouetted by the sinking sun's peach-colored light. The Tonkawa had thrown the leather back on them. Stardust's mane blazed amber. "I swallowed some air," Hawk continued, " 'fore dropping that buck was holding yer mount." He gestured toward the warrior sprawled over Texas' body. "That's how come this 'un came close."

"I'm obliged," said Renald. He summoned his horse with a rousing cavalry call—*"Heohhhhh!"*

Stardust whinnied. Catching sight of his rider about seventy feet down, he stepped over the body heaped at his hooves and started for him, followed faithfully by the mule.

"Shame about Texas," Hawk remarked. "I warned him not to draw on you."

"He didn't," said Renald. "He did his duty."

At his side, Laura Little looked proud of herself. "*I* killed him."

"That so?" said Hawk. "You murdered him, you mean."

She regarded the bodies. "Days back they butchered the band I was riding with and *ate them*. He was head of the party."

"Save that fer the court. Texas died in the service of the U.S. Cavalry." He spit tobacco. "Where'd you get yerself a revolver?"

Setting her chin to chest, she raised her guarded eyes without remark.

He eyed Renald critically. "Good you took it back 'fore *I* fell on this pile."

Without waiting for a reaction, he pried the topmost body off with his rifle barrel. They all stepped back to avoid the blood splatter. Exposed was Texas, eyes glazed, bloodstained tunic glued to his torso. Frozen on his face was that look of disbelief. Hawk bent over the body and worked his hand into one of the hip pockets. He ripped out the envelope containing Texas' pay and parted the flap to expose a wad of cash. "Lookee here! Not just three months' pay, but a fine wage besides."

Renald was disconsolate, speechless.

Hawk shoved the envelope into his vest. "Let's bury him."

"Is there time for that?" Laura Little chirped.

Each man gripped a shoulder, and together they heaved Texas off the remains lying crosswise beneath. The buffalo hunter set to arranging the body—boots facing west, left arm straightened against his torso, right arm bent at the elbow, and right hand placed over his chest wound. With flicks of his fingers he clicked Texas' mouth shut and rolled his eyelids closed. Last, he clawed the ground and sprinkled some dirt on the body. Then he righted himself and reached for his rifle. Renald nodded with admiration.

Hawk tapped up his hat, explaining, "Watched him do it over his chief and brother back there ..."

"His brother?"

"That's what he said."

"He could've killed me for that."

Hawk shouldered the Henry. "Maybe he shoulda tried."

Renald frowned, regarding the body. He grasped a fold of the blanket torn down by Texas' fall and locked eyes with Laura Little, bitterly. "Last chance to take his scalp. You earned it."

She turned away, and he laid the sheet gently over Texas, covering the Indian's face. "Somebody's gonna be shivering tonight," he told her, "and it ain't me."

With Texas' burial behind them, their attention was drawn to the clip-clops of horse and mule on their windy way down to their spot, once as plain as any other in these parts but today marked by a half dozen bloodied bodies. To the weary, after a morning of gunfire and killing, those plodding steps soothed like wind charms, a sensation experienced but momentarily. A roar of hoofbeats arose, the rocky bowl an echo chamber. Laura Little's eyes darted here and there. She spun around with a look of distress. "More Tonk!"

"Relax, lady," Hawk groaned. "Them's Comanche."

"How do you reckon?"

"For one thing, they're approaching from the north." He pinched the tattered brim of his hat. "My compliments, Captain."

"Retired," said Renald.

A smile lit up her face, and, after expanding it to Renald, she showed them both her back. As she stepped away, the men admired her figure in those riding pants, but when she promptly began making animal calls toward the horizon, they caught themselves, brows furrowing.

"She's plum gone native," said Hawk. "Now what?"

Below their heels, the earth began to tremble. Renald responded to Hawk's stare. "You best go."

The hide man brought his rifle off his shoulder, bouncing the barrel in his left palm. "I sure ain't returning empty-handed! Anyhow, it's safer us riding together—with you my prisoner in case we encounter any Tonkaways. That's enough fer me."

Renald allowed himself an amused grin. Hawk couldn't feasibly take him prisoner any more than the hide man could convince him to ride back to Sill free. And to pretend to be a prisoner, disarmed and bound, was to be one.

"I stick with her," he answered.

Hawk was stunned. "What fer? It's over—ain't it?" He leaned in. "Scott, the army's close at hand. Columns from all directions are converging on the area, cleaning out every rat's nest they find. Colonel Mackenzie's leading *three* from Fort Concho, Colonel Buell's marching from Fort Griffin, Colonel Miles from Kansas, and Major Price is marching from New Mexico. We'll rendezvous with 10th Troop a day behind us. You've overshot the mark here. The Comanche camp's in Double Barrel Gorge."

"What?"

"That's how come Texas enlisted. Davidson's diverting from North Scalp. He'll get there first."

Renald looked troubled. Davidson might reach the Comanche camp before *he* did. "When he raids into it, the hostages lose their value," he said. "Those Hermann boys could be killed outright." But he was really thinking of another boy.

"They who you was sent out fer?"

"Another redeemer is assigned to Apache and Arapaho lands."

"Well, I saw them orders—yer to return with me. I got my orders too."

"What sort of a bounty is Black Jack paying out? Scout pay ain't enough for a man like you. Or are the buffalo even worse off than I thought?"

Hawk sounded proud. "Army and injun meat buyer. Five years, exclusive. When the frontier opens."

Renald waved him quiet. "Spare me ..."

A dust boil appeared above the rocky eminence toward which Laura Little had gravitated. Over his shoulder, Renald said, "This is your last chance to hightail it. No telling what they'll do."

The old horse soldier mulled it over, expression hidden by the brim of his hat. First Texas' obstinacy, and now Scott's? At last, he said, "I throw in with you."

"With me?"

"She's already shot down one agent of the U.S. government. What's one more? I ride away without you, I'll soon have Comanche biting my butt. No, sir. She protects you, and you protect me. You don't keep me alive, you got no witness to her admission *she* shot Texas."

Hawk had a point. Renald was about to respond when Stardust nearly toppled him with a show of affection, pressing him with his spongy muzzle and snorting in his ear. After a cold, lonely night and a morning hobbled in the shade of an overhang, and finally his capture by a bare-skinned stranger who'd handled him roughly and stood him in the sweltering sun, the animal showed an almost canine rush of excitement for his owner. Renald, holding himself steady in his boots, ran his hand over Stardust's white-patched brow and rubbed his cheeks before the horse, sensing danger, pinned back his ears. Renald raised his eyes while furtively retrieving his last box of cartridges from the saddlebag. Hawk noticed.

In a steady line, eight mounted fighting men swept onto the ridge above, grasping lances, bows, coup sticks, and a saddle gun or two. Notably, their beasts packed gear sacks. One of the figures, atop a pale horse, wore a great headdress, feathered all the way down the back.

"Talking Moon?" asked Hawk.

Renald shook his head. "If he were Quahada he'd be wearing antlers."

The leader did not signal attack. Halting their animals, they surveyed the carnage surrounding the white men. Satisfied all the enemy braves had been vanquished, the party filed down to level ground and formed a southeast-facing line opposite the men and woman. Some braves rode completely bareback, others on colorful saddle blankets. Simple breechcloths adorned their tattooed bodies. Their hair was braided over their shoulders, and, in what was called a scalp lock, they wore a single feather above the brow secured by a third, thinner braiding. Red-dyed feathers decorated the most proven warriors. Unlike his men, the chief, center, was clothed in an embroidered tunic in the southern style and wore fringe-beaded earrings of turquoise and coral. He rode his varnish roan out a few steps.

Laura Little approached him, talking forcefully. His silence meanwhile—perhaps it was speechlessness—affirmed the power of her presence. Behind him, the others exchanged looks as she told her story.

As for Renald and Hawk, they were bracing for gunplay when another round of hoofbeats arose, fainter to start and thus better pinpointed. "Could be riders breaking off from that horse trail back of us," Hawk conjectured—correctly, as it turned out. "Tonkaways?"

"If they are, we'll be caught in the crossfire," Renald answered. "But notice those bucks ain't alarmed. They're expecting others."

The chief slid down to greet Laura Little. He offered her water from a simple paunch bag and a bite of something from an embroidered rations sack. They commenced talking animatedly, with familiarity, making numerous references to the white men whom they interestingly called *gringos,* not *taiboo nuu.* Renald and Hawk strained to hear them through the drum of hoof falls and to understand the rapidly spoken tongue. Equally attentive were the fighting men left and right who leaned in, faces, chests, and arms illustrated with war paint.

"Did you get that about the relief station?" Renald asked Hawk. "He seems to know about near everything."

"Seems more breakouts took the same route. I reckon they was dogging me and Texas."

"Wouldn't be hard to do—that is, with your spitting tobacco all the way. But it's the Tonk war party that must've really worried them. They broke off somewhere to raise the alarm."

"This party is equipped for travel," Hawk observed. "Why?"

"They come from the southern borderlands. Notice their saddle blankets—Penateka, not Quahada. *Listen*. She's explaining *your* presence …"

The chief interrupted Laura Little and began motioning aggressively their way.

"I don't like the way he's firing looks at me," Hawk muttered. "Let's you and me whip our weight in wildcats. I'll take the four to the right."

Renald regarded him with amusement. "It's not that we can't lick 'em. But when we spin to face the others she could grab herself a rifle and backshoot us."

"I reckon she would. So I'll disarm her while you spin …"

"Keep your weapon holstered. That shows more courage—for the present."

They watched in astonishment as the plumed chief bent his knees and locked his hands. Supporting her boot, he lifted Laura Little onto his mount. As she raised both hands to collect her hair and stow it inside her hat, her jutting chest drew their attention.

"Woo-wee," exclaimed Hawk from his low angle. "That's plum all over the place beauty, ain't it? When I came man-age, my daddy told me to stay clear away from that type."

Renald replied, "I bet they stayed clear away from you too."

Hawk chuckled, revealing a few whiskey-colored choppers flecked with tobacco. "Aw, I'm not so ugly bathed and shaved." He spit. "She's sure got you hog-tied! You gave her the gun and she used it against you. Now lookee who's on top."

As Laura Little took the reins, the chief stripped a booted rifle from the horse. They traded more words. She told him something very assertively, which drew a hostile response. They debated, their words lost in the rising hoof rumble.

"Can you make out what they're saying?" Hawk was worried.

"Whatever it is, he seems to have won this point."

The chief had wheeled around and started for them, scowling. Behind him, the rest of his party readied themselves on their mounts with their weapons.

Renald eyed Hawk. "Scared?"

"Same as you."

Renald loosened his muscles. By dropping the Winchester and drawing his sidearm he could empty the cylinder with pin-point accuracy for every two shots fired from a lever-action rifle. To finish the job, he'd drop to a knee and unleash the Winchester. He presumed Hawk would adopt the same tactics if he was fast. The big man's level of confidence suggested he was.

The chief was two or three paces away when Laura Little told them, "They want your mule and the Tonk's horse."

Hawk's shoulders collapsed. "There's half a dozen mounts yonder on the prairie! How come yer taking this one?"

"We're taking that one *too*. The others are being brought up." That explained the earthquake.

The chief, a man whose height was greatly assisted by his headdress, avoided eye contact now that he was an arm's distance from Hawk—either unwilling to look up at the *taiboo* or—could it be?—a show of respect. Though not young, he had a spring in his step and, after strapping the fringed scabbard onto the pinto, swung nimbly into the saddle and eased back on the reins. But the animal wasn't going to make it easy for him. Shrinking back, she tried to get above the bit, then snorted, reared, and neighed in protest. Jumpy beast and headdressed rider looked like some Frontier Day attraction.

Hawk grinned with pleasure, remarking, "That Tonkaway mount sure don't like to sit Comanche!"

While the chief struggled with the unruly animal, Hawk got into his own saddle. He put his rifle away and, like Renald standing below him, enjoyed the show. Finally, the chief brought the feisty horse aside Hawk's and extended a hand.

"What does he want? A handshake?"

"He wants that currency meant for the Tonkawa," answered Laura Little. "I added it as a deal sweetener."

A deal sweetener? Renald grimaced. Just yesterday he'd used the term with her. The woman knew how to adapt.

Hawk's reaction was to spit tobacco with contempt.

"Don't make me take it," said the chief in flawless English.

Renald narrowed his eyes. Silence. Wonder. Worry. "Let's not have any trouble, Hawk. Give it to him."

"He wanted your weapons too," she said, "but I insisted you'll need them on the way back."

"That's a helluva good deal, Hawk."

Exasperated, Hawk dug into his vest. With the envelope in hand, the chief reversed the horse but stayed close. Now Laura Little was barking orders at his men to gather the weapons, ammunition, and the stuff inside the cave—as if they needed to be told, thought Renald. They'd arrived on the scene with mostly stone age weapons but would ride away with repeaters to a man, and then some. They jumped to obey her, dispersing on their mounts, the whole scene chaotic with movement. Throughout, Renald remained resignedly beside Stardust, rifle tucked under his arm. All the while he combed his knowledge, his memories for the identity of this English-speaking Penateka chief.

From his saddle, Hawk grumbled, "They're collecting them guns fer use against the cavalry, *Captain* ..."

Laura Little advanced her cool mount, halting at Renald's feet. Her eyes settled on him with queenly comportment. "Scott, you've reunited me with my people. I am Watsi-ni Nuena again—Whispering Wind."

Craning his neck, he replied, "Should you survive what's to come, in a short while you'll be Laura Little again—back in Fort Worth."

She glanced at the chief, who was busy asserting his authority over the barn-sour animal. "If my son is with me, I could live with that."

Renald hesitated, surprised. "I ride back alone, I'm liable to be court-martialed."

"Ride with me, and worse awaits you. My husband will not send you back to the army knowing his location."

"Funny you didn't raise that concern before. But I'll take that chance for those missing boys."

Laura Little seemed to think it over. She held out her hand.

He was suspicious. "Is that a handshake you're offering or you want something?"

"My pistol. I'm a silly sight with this holster bereft."

Hawk chimed in, "Only because of that?"

Renald paused. Why should she want the short gun, protected as she was by mounted warriors? Surrounded by them himself, he could hardly withhold it. He drew the weapon from the small of his back, gave it a lead-pusher's whirl, and held it grip-up to her.

Hawk was astonished. "Restoring her weapon? Yer as loco as she is!"

"Watch your words," she snapped, nodding toward the chief. "Any more lip from you, I'll tell him you hunt buffalo." She holstered the gun. Then, eyeing Renald, she said, "I'll always wonder how Stardust got his name, Scott."

Renald found himself suppressing a grin. The woman sure had pluck. "I'm sure you will," he answered, sheathing his Winchester. He stepped into the saddle and Stardust whinnied with delight, stamping his hooves. "Take me to Talking Moon," he told Laura Little. "I've killed his enemies and saved his wife. Maybe he'll listen."

"My husband is Iron Mountain's son, but he is not like Iron Mountain."

"Maybe there's elders who can reason with him. Red Bear ..."

"I met Bad Eagle and Wild Horse on the reservation. He won't even talk to them. *He's had a vision.*"

"Spare me," replied Renald.

The echoing hoof thunder increased to a roar. On the ridge, riders leading empty mounts began to appear in a northward procession, dotting a gunmetal-grey sky. The warriors exchanged triumphant hoots and yelps with the chief and his party below.

Hawk was shaking his head. "What a haul! They got all them Tonk repeaters too." As if Laura Little wasn't there, he told Renald, "We best warn the horse soldiers."

"You do that," she said, "and tell them to look out for me and my boy. Remember who my uncle is."

"Well, that takes it ..." gasped Renald.

Hawk snorted with disgust. "Suddenly her family matters!"

Powerless except to commit more bloodshed at terrific odds, they must turn tail. Renald envisioned himself under escort to the guardhouse at Fort Sill, that lonesome days-long journey in the opposite direction while the army advanced to engage the enemy—the boy's life hanging in the balance. He squeezed his gun hand into a white-knuckled fist.

Rotating toward Hawk, he said, "I throw in with you."

Laura Little exposed her clean teeth in a smile that brought color to her cheeks. Her expression settled. "You've endured hardship for me, Scott. I'm grateful."

"I got my reasons."

The chief advanced his new mount, holding her steady. *"Bastante!"* he growled at Laura Little. In English, "Enough with the *gringos.*"

It came together for Renald. He snapped his fingers. "You're the *mestizo* chief!"

"Mixed, yes. Many of us are mixed."

Looking past their paint, Renald did indeed note the lighter skin of some warriors, the lower cheekbones, hair more brown than black. "Your mother was Mexican," he continued with wonder, "and your father was the great Penateka Santa Anna!"

"Correcto. I am Carne Muerto."

"Chief *Dead Meat?*" exclaimed Hawk. "You must be joking."

Renald waved off his interference. "I was expecting Quahada out here, not Penateka. You're far from home. Joining Talking Moon?"

"Maybe."

To Hawk, Renald explained, "Rip Ford captured him as a young man and held him for trade."

The chief raised his chin. "He kept me one year."

"First at Fort McIntosh, then at Merrill. I remember. You were treated well."

"Rip thought my father lived."

"That's sure what you wanted him to believe. Gave you value. Your mother came for you but was turned away. I remember that too. You escaped. So now you're combining with the Quahada. What a shame. The Penateka were cooperative. We called your father the peace chief. The fathers made peace, the sons make war."

"Not all believe Indian medicine has returned ... will return. Most of our men are still back at the Pecos with Chief Tosahwi. I come to talk."

"The army wants to talk to chiefs who want to talk." Renald nodded northward. "Know where you're going?"

"Más o menos."

"You could take me along as your guide."

"Indians using a white guide?" Carne Muerto shook his head. "We know what to look for." Next he shouted orders at his men regarding the white men's transit. Then to Renald, "You see Rip, offer him my *recuerdos.*"

"I will if I get the chance."

"Here is your chance," said the chief. "My men will watch you cross the Llano in the direction of the sunrise."

"You'll understand if I don't quite thank you for that."

"It's your privilege. You are Captain Renald."

"Was," he replied. "Well then, I reckon that concludes our business, doesn't it?" He swung Stardust alongside Laura Little. "Come time when that bugle sounds, don't bite, and for

godsakes don't shoot. Just shield your son with that fair hair of yours. Keep it washed."

He pinched the brim of his hat, then reined Stardust around.

* * *

Six braves provided them silent escort off Survivor's Bluff. The air had chilled, and the fighting men now wore buckskins over their broad, thick torsos. Halting their animals at the bottom of the horse trail, this was the moment when the white men must trust in the hostiles, separated from their chief as they were, or reach for their guns. Perhaps sensing their apprehension, one of the braves rode out in front. He extended his hand toward the open tablelands of the Staked Plain, awash in the lavenders and greys of dusk. *"No tengan miedo,"* he said—"Have no fear."

After trading wary glances, the two white men rode past him onto the open range.

Part IV

Double Barrel Gorge

Chapter Ten

In civilian life these old troopers were far from friends, but for all their contrasts they shared the mutual respect of decorated soldiers turned solitary plainsmen, a kind of kinship. More, in today's contest of wits and bravery they had earned each other's admiration. Trouble was, they were riding back without the woman—and for Renald, without her son too. He'd always returned with somebody. This time he wasn't even leading.

Intent on avoiding the remains of the fallen Tonkawa and their chief's shallow grave, they rode clear around that place in a northerly arc, contemplating what to do, each man feeling he'd come away with almost nothing but his life and reluctant to face a disappointed Lieutenant Colonel Davidson. Hawk rode first while Renald hung his head, barely conscious of Stardust's hoof falls. Against the odds he had succeeded at restoring Laura Little to the Comanche, yet he was riding away without any trace of satisfaction. All those Tonkawa dead, Texas killed, and the child still in danger.

Trotting dumbly away from the butte as it faded into the night, he imagined son and mother in tearful embrace before the pointed village lodges. He saw the boy's brown face buried in her chest, his raven black falls. He could almost feel the gorge's crisp air, hear the trickle of its stream, and smell the campfire smoke. Murkier inventions followed of Laura reuniting with her husband. Uncontrollably, Renald saw a lustful Talking Moon repossessing her in some dark and drafty tepee. How would she react when he ordered her down? If willing, she was as savage as he. If unwilling, she'd be savaged by him. One way or another she would descend again into barbarism.

The picture of Laura sharing that mat, those embraces, put his mind in a dreary place from which there might've been no rescue; but then he recalled her admission—her plea?—that she could live with her son in Fort Worth. His hope renewed. She'd never spoken of missing Talking Moon, never even defended him. In all their time together Renald never once saw her pray to the Great Spirit or make offerings of any sort. Her true attachment was to her son, not to the tribe.

Again he began to conjecture what he might accomplish—prevent—if he confronted Talking Moon.

When darkness fell upon the Llano they were just halfway across the windswept divide between Survivor's Bluff and their intended night sanctuary in the basin. Hawk reined his horse, heeding the stars. Renald followed his lead, having anticipated this moment. The two men faced each other in the moonlight.

The bigger man broke the tension. "Notice how them braves escorted us rode back up the trail instead of around the butte?"

"Yes, I did."

"Means they're spending the night atop."

"Least some of it ... some of them."

Hawk leaned back, straining saddle leather. "How 'bout you and me ride after her?"

Renald shook his head. "We wouldn't stand a chance. He'll have sentries posted."

"No doubt he will. I mean, we attrit them same as you done the Tonkaways. Only we start when they ride *off* the butte, back-facing us—in the morrow."

"Supposing they set out before dawn?"

"Creeping up on animals is my business. We follow 'em at a safe remove. Time comes, I unleash my Sharps. When they get us back in range the odds'll be even."

Renald shuddered at the image of Comanche riders bearing down on them, firing from horseback. "Not interested," he said.

"Not interested? Them's Comanche, Scott. Same as robbed you of yer wife. How come you won't bushwhack 'em like you bushwhacked us Yankees in the war?"

"I got a reason," Renald replied with irritation.

"The woman?" Hawk responded, misunderstanding. "We can shoot around her."

"Without her son in the bargain, I ain't interested." Here was his chance. "Listen, Hawk, if I ride alone and reach the elders I can get myself admitted to camp. I'll find it before Carne Muerto does. Remember what he said about knowing what to look for? If the Quahada are in Double Barrel Gorge, it figures their marker is the rock itself. Double Barrel Rock. It sticks out like two thumbs."

The moonglow blinked on Hawk's brow as he nodded. "He's using the Spanish horse trail. It runs due north. So you reckon he'll enter the gorge from the far west and ride eastward, not to miss anything."

"Exactly. Starting from here, I can make it in half the time ..."

"Scott, ain't I just saved you getting scalped? This time you'd be relying on the army to rescue you—a colored troop at that. If yer that gutty, you oughta finish the job with me here and now."

"The job, as you call it, ain't finished till the boy is mine."

"Yers?" Hawk spit tobacco. "Just whatd'ya mean by that?"

"He's my blood, Hawk."

"Yer blood?"

"Talking Moon's a half blood. His mother was a Texican."

Hawk's surprise was hidden by the shadows under his brow. He tried to put it together. "You telling me yer wife wasn't killed in that fire?"

Renald swallowed. "She was. It was my sister they took."

"Yer sister?"

"I knew one of them was taken. The remains didn't say which. Just before you showed, Laura recognized her in a picture I carry."

Hawk's mouth cracked open as he tried to make sense of it, his night-grey teeth countable among the gaps. "Jesus," he groaned. "That'd make Talking Moon yer nephew!" He did some math with his fingers. "And his son near full-blooded white!"

"He's six years old and speaks English, she says."

Hawk sniggered. "*Mine*, he says, *mine! The boy's mine.* Well, you sure got a claim to him! His father's a hostile, and his mother's mental. But you didn't tell her, did you?"

"I meant to," said Renald. "Then I thought better of it."

"You done right! She plugs men get between. You got yerself some family, turns out! Or should I say, *some family?*"

"What're we going to do about it?"

Hawk blew a breath. "I get the feeling you're about to tell me."

"One of us needs to alert Davidson the Penateka are combining with the Quahada, that they're packing repeaters. Meantime, I can attempt to negotiate a truce from the inside."

Hawk replied, "You wanna negotiate a peace, safer doing it from the outside."

"I can't count on Black Jack keeping me around."

" 'Cause yer Johnny Reb Renald, and them's a colored troop."

"With Tonkawa scouts," Renald added.

Hawk pointed at the knife strapped to Renald's chest, between the lapels of his jacket. "That sure ain't gonna help you none."

"It might with the Comanche. Look, I may be a *taiboo*, but I'm Talking Moon's uncle. The Comanche must respect their elder kinsman."

"Eh, he'll scalp you at the first bugle call."

"Maybe. But negotiations are *my* business. Give me a chance."

A gust arose, chilling the men through their clothing. Hawk filled his lungs with a long drag of air. "Scott, I let you go, Black Jack'll tan my hide."

"Not if events prove you did right. Let me go, Hawk …"

The big man crossed his hands over the saddle horn and sat with absolute stillness for a good minute while his mount shifted her weight. Looking here and there into the moonlit expanse, he seemed to be playing out different scenarios in his mind.

Finally, he fixed Renald crossways. "Packing enough water fer the journey?"

Lighting up with a toothy smile, Renald cut the air with his two-fingered salute. He reversed Stardust into the darkness. In a whirl, man and horse were gone.

* * *

As sunrise swept across the land like a grass fire, the desolate alkaline flats of the Llano Estacado began to recede behind them. Step by step Renald and Stardust penetrated more fertile terrain. First, patches of yucca practically sprouted from the earth before their eyes, then sand sage, colorful Apache plume, and tall warm-season grass, all under the bluest sky the season could offer. Pushing their way through the knee-high grama, a full-fledged stream rolled out in front of them, beyond it another expanse of brushlands and the first juniper and cottonwood Renald had seen in days. Above the treetops a broad outlying stone parapet loomed dark and mysterious, gateway to Double Barrel Gorge.

Gone were the unsettling thoughts that had occupied him all night and morning, vanquished by the unfolding beauty and telltale sounds of hospitable country—water rushing over stone, buzzing and birdsong, the drumming of a yellow-bellied sapsucker. Urgent though his mission was, the glittering stream offered a precious opportunity to replenish himself and his animal. Stardust whinnied at the presence of water, stamping his hooves. His rider glanced around. Should they rest and risk discovery? Unless buffalo were close, it was unlikely a hunting party would venture so far from the comparative safety of the gorge, if that was indeed where the Quahada had encamped.

Renald would take the chance. He dismounted and relieved his deserving horse of the weight of his saddle and gear. With a tap on the beast's rear, he sent Stardust into the sock-high creek to drink his fill. Sensing its shallowness, the dust-matted sorrel folded his legs and lay momentarily on his side before rising to shake off the water. Hands on hips, Renald admired his graceful animal, the sheen restored to his copper-red coat. From days of parched hardship on the Llano to a spring-water renewal—such was the changeable, paradoxical nature of the country. Rousing himself, he got free of his own trappings and rinsed and wrung out his clothes in the stream, setting shirt, socks, and underthings out to dry. Next he partook of the waters, lying on his back against smooth and slippery stones and letting the current, icy near its source, run transparently over his weary body. He rose on his elbows, his beard sandpaper-scratchy against his neck, and eyed his saddlebags with a tempting thought. A minute later he was squatted beside the creek with a straight razor and clump of soap, shaving four days' growth clean. Reflected, his sun-baked face looked as dark as Stardust's coat, his sun-bleached hair as light as his horse's mane.

With a hungry snort Stardust climbed onto the opposite bank, where at once he set to grazing on the abundant grass. Meantime, Renald, bare but for his hat, dug into yet another tinny meal under the shade of a cottonwood. Chewing the embalmed beef, he wondered how many more days would pass till he could get some steak and potatoes back at the fort. Would they serve him such a meal in the guardhouse? Yawning, he felt the untold hours of sleep lost in recent days. The dangers toward which he was riding required agility of mind and muscle, and there was no telling if a night's rest would come between now and then. Only Stardust's relative vigor, following his rest on the butte, had kept them going.

Renald squinted aloft through the leaves. The sun was yet to hang high. He eased back and let his eyelids shutter down. With a last flicker of strength, he shielded his face with his hat. A smile on his lips, he yielded to slumber.

* * *

Stardust was nibbling at his ear. With a quick movement, Renald swiped his hat away and looked straight into his horse's blinking, amber eye. Stiffly, he got to his feet, checking the sun's position and ascertaining he'd dozed too long. Glancing down at his nakedness, he shook his head. Had an Indian party happened upon him, he sure would've been a sight, splayed exposed on his back, face covered, perhaps the victim of some native torture. Moving fast, he retrieved his now crisp garments from the waterside and got dressed. With the seat of his pants pressed against a rock, he pulled his boots on. He buckled his gun belt, tied down the holster, and, remembering, kicked dirt over the empty food tin. Finally, he reached for Stardust's saddle.

After their long repose, both rider and horse—groomed, satiated, and refitted—headed into the brushlands beyond the opposite bank, where the regular draft had bent the yellow grama eastward in a static sway. It was places like this that counted among the last refuges of the last herds of bison. Here Renald spotted nothing bigger than the odd wild turkey. If only he could roast one up.

Soon they entered the welcoming patchwork shade of a juniper grove, alive with grinding cicadas, buzzing flies, fiddling crickets, and hopping lizards as big as a boy's forearm. Through the leaves and branches, the stone escarpment towered ahead in scarlet and lavender, horizontally chalked. Renald dismounted for their ascent of it. By mid-afternoon they were atop the southern wall of the V-shaped gorge, at the bottom of which—eight hundred feet below—a thin Red River tributary zigzagged silently through jagged rocky steps. Peering eastward across the divide to where the stream jackknifed, he caught sight of its telltale marker—a two-pronged natural rock formation, eighty feet high, that to thirsty conquistadors had once resembled a pair of sherry casks. Though not distant as the bird flies, reaching it would take hours no matter which course they followed, such was the roughness of the terrain both up here and down below. From where Stardust stood, they could switchback to the bottom and head downstream, but following the stream might jeopardize the element of surprise on which Renald's penetration of the village relied. Instead, he decided to stick to high ground, where a lone rider could move undetected among the rocks, keeping an eye out all the while for rising smoke. Mindful of the toll such uneven ground would take on his mount's joints, he walked Stardust as much as he rode him, scanning the trail for tracks that might lead them to the Comanche camp. From time to time rider and horse sheltered in the shade of a crevice or a scrawny tree. Grazing material was scarce, and Stardust's fodder was running short. Renald snacked on jerky and hardtack, saving his last tin for supper.

As the sun dipped low in the west, shadows spilled from everything, even the slightest brittle weed, and after a while, where the stone-shard path led into a soft-ground trail, a procession of darkened hoof marks suddenly emerged. Leading Stardust, he lowered himself onto one knee and counted a party of four or five in them. With the back of his ungloved hand he patted the sides of the shod and unshod tracks, finding them equally grainy, yet to be toughened by night chill. He regained his mount and chirruped Stardust forward with caution.

The blaze of sundown slashed the sandstone into a bloodbath of vibrant color until its fireball slipped below the horizon and the greys of dusk rolled toward them through the gorge like a flash flood. Rider and horse followed the trail as it worked its way toward the riverbed. Stardust pricked back his ears at their first encounter with horse droppings, still moist at his hooves. Renald pulled rein. "Easy, boy," he whispered, patting his animal's neck. "We're following too close." He studied the darkening ravine walls. This was where he would hunker down. Barring freak rainfall, the tracks of the party ahead would remain readable at dawn, even in the anticipated morning mist under whose cover Renald was intent on slipping close to camp, refreshed from a night's sleep.

Despite Renald's unintended slumber back there, Carne Muerto must still be at least half a day behind. There were no speedy routes through the treacherous gorge, and the night multiplied its dangers manyfold to men with mounts.

Supposing, for the moment, the band ahead was the one that had tracked Hawk and alerted Carne Muerto, he wondered how much they knew. Carne Muerto had arrived on the scene wearing war paint, expecting to fight a large party of Tonkawa. That suggested the alerting party must've broken away from the chase well before Survivor's Bluff, ignorant of who was being pursued or the resultant bloodshed. Should Renald confront Talking Moon below, the revelation of Laura Little's transit might remain his to make when it became prudent. Beyond that, speculation was useless.

He dismounted, led Stardust off the trail, and chose a patch of ground suitable for making camp, fragrant sumac and saltbush providing the surrounding cover. Reaching into his bags, he found the remaining horse meal, a disappointing snack for his animal following this morning's wild grass feast. Nevertheless, Stardust ate obediently from his hands. From a saddlebag Renald produced the tin of beef and crossed his legs at Stardust's hooves. The last can-cold meal. Weighing it in his grasp, he wondered if his next meal would be served up by angels, devils, or a Comanche squaw. So long as it was hot, it didn't matter.

While the katydids awakened from their day slumber, he unrolled his bed and made a pillow of the saddle. When it was dark he smelled the campfires, heard faraway voices and occasional laughter, horse cries. He'd cut short his approach just in time. Daylight would suit his purposes. He must make the most of the night. Crossing his arms over his chest, pistol in hand, he beheld the blinking stars.

A stridulating chorus lulled him to sleep—with his boots on.

Chapter Eleven

Dawn revealed the blanket of fog Renald had expected. At first he could scarcely see beyond his glove, and he might've had cotton in his ears for all he could hear around him, the damper absorbing sound and odor alike. Sitting cross-legged on his mat, he longed for the coffee he'd left strapped to the mule. With plenty of luck he might enjoy a hot cup tonight—mule, coffee, and kettle were all making their way back to him.

When visibility allowed he set out on foot, keeping a tight hold of Stardust and double-checking the trail as they went. Careful not to slip on the dewy stones, they made slow progress. Even after an hour's descent the stream remained all but hidden behind veils of mist drifting across the basin, the exact location of the Indian village still unknown. The sun's persistent eye eventually peeked through, and, as if it had given the order, the fog rose like ruffled curtains at a theater show. Revealed between there and here was a distributary rivulet undetected from the summit. Over the ages it had carved out a shallow but wide arroyo that curved all the way back to the main vessel, the junction located just below Double Barrel Rock. Perfect.

Minutes later, mounted, he sidestepped down the slope, the dew-sodden topsoil slipping in thick ripples like lumpy flapjack batter. When they reached the gully bottom, he pointed Stardust upstream and paused him. All was quiet but for the trickling water. Before them the arcing walls, dotted haphazardly with mesquite and ocotillo, resembled a pianola's perforated rolls. Above and throughout the greater gorge, lofty vestiges of mist soared into the brightening sky. His eyes scanned side to side. If a sentry was lying in wait somewhere ahead, at any moment he might reveal himself with a twang of bowstring. Renald stuffed his right glove into a side pocket, pulled his Winchester, and jacked the finger lever—a noise that pricked Stardust's sensitive ears and maybe others, for all he knew. He held the reins in his glove and the rifle in his bare hand. He leaned the barrel across his left shoulder, parted his lips, and blew warmth on his knuckles.

He whispered to Stardust, "Here on I'm sure gonna work you, sweetheart." It was his first utterance since yesterday, and his animal responded by swinging his head around and eying him with curiosity. If any mount could be relied on, it was Stardust. Renald lovingly rubbed his horse's underside with his boots. Somehow, they would get through this. He nudged him forward across the creek.

Renald felt the danger from his knees to his neck. Never had he approached an enemy camp during hostilities unless backed by a troop column, and while he was confident a thinking brave wouldn't attack him outright, there were plenty of brash ones out there, eager for scalps. Contact with one kind or the other was imminent. Likely, Talking Moon had instructed his warriors to use traditional weapons near their stronghold, rather than the rifle. A gunshot's crack would roar through the gorge—who knew how far. Renald kept Stardust at a sixty-yard remove from the opposite side, beyond the accurate range of a bow and arrow, so near the curve of the wall, in fact, that the odd bramble scraped his pant leg. They pushed forward around the bend, the far wall snaking toward them as if animated.

Before the mouth of the arroyo the two walls aligned. From the gap between blew a draft that caused Renald to blink and Stardust's nostrils to flare as he clopped nearer and nearer. With the patch of light widening to the eye the monotonous backdrop gained depth and detail. Ochre and red hues emerged from the towering wall to the north. Reaching the opening, Renald detected what Stardust had already sensed—the presence of livestock around the corner. It was time to put his rifle away. Only his wits could protect them now.

Once again he was advancing Stardust from a place of concealment into the open, but this time the danger was as real as the rock's barrel-chested twin prongs that loomed overhead like all-seeing guards. Renald jogged the reins to the right.

A stone's throw away, at the shaded base of a stepped overhang, thronged the largest pony herd Renald had seen in a long time, bigger than any buffalo herd left in dry country. Mustangs, thoroughbreds, saddlers, Arabians, and Palouse— some, like the ferals, seized wild; others acquired by raid or trade. Numbering possibly over a thousand head, it was the treasure trove of the Comanche nation, what was left of it. To pen them off, the Indians had caused a rockslide and rolled the boulders into a semicircle around the wall. Between the rocks, wooden stakes had been driven into the ground, connected by sinews to form a fence too weak to contain the herd if it got jumpy. If a warrior existed for even half the horses, the odds were dismal for any cavalry battalion unless the Comanche were ambuscaded right here, the animals spooked into stampede. But if that transpired, many a woman and child would die in the doing.

Next lay the village itself, partially glimpsed from this vantage point but clearly of magnificent proportions. Renald patted Stardust's withers. "Here goes, sweetheart ..."

He took a deep breath and signaled the horse forward. They trotted up the riverbed opposite the pen. No sentries were posted anywhere that he could see, perhaps because the army avoided ravine bottoms for fear of ambush. The Comanche normally avoided them too, for the same reason. This hideout, however, provided retreat routes to both the forbidding Llano and the labyrinthine Palo Duro, while offering water and wild birds for the tribe and plenty of sweetgrass upstream for the animals. Passing the pen, Renald noted how the camp was set back against a high sandstone shelf that concealed it from a northerly view into the gorge. He gawked, awestruck, at its size and organization. Like tents in a military camp, the tepees and wikiups were uniformly distanced, five across and as deep as the eye could see till the haze swallowed them. This broke with the tradition of organizing a village in tribal circles or circles for each band. If the village extended to the dramatic convergence of the walls, there could be two thousand inhabitants, even more. Faint traces of smoke rose here and there into the fiery sky, a draft circulating the scent of smoldering embers. Renald detected no movement at all. The village was sleeping late.

He must reach Red Bear.

Given the untraditional layout, he surmised the chiefs' lodges would be situated in the middle of camp, whether that be forty or sixty deep. He was partly right. Once somebody sounded the alarm, Stardust must fly there. For now, Renald kept him at a quiet trot, the murmuring stream washing over his footfalls. To his right he regarded the conical lodges and domed rooms, the cook tents, and the picketed mounts fanning the air with their tails, a normalcy he was about to shatter. To soothe his nerves, and maybe those of his animal too, he recited a common marching hymn under his breath:

> "Round her neck she wears a yeller ribbon,
> She wears it in the winter and the summer so they say,
> If you ask her 'Why the decoration?'
> She'll say 'It's fur my lover who is fur, fur away.'
> Fur away, Fur away!
> She'll say 'It's fur my lover who is fur, fur away!' "

They passed ten lodges before the camp dogs howled alarm and lunged into snarling pursuit. Loosening his jaw, Renald kicked Stardust into a gallop. Dogs could be outrun, but human commotion was already spreading faster than pounding hooves could take them. Cries were going up everywhere, flap doors opening to reveal blanketed, robed, and half-naked figures. As the men grabbed their weapons and vaulted onto their mounts, the women gathered their curious children.

Renald twisted back to see the whooping, howling warriors heeling their animals forward and drawing their bows. Unburdened by saddlebags, the native mounts would gain rapidly on Stardust. Meantime, dogs spilled in from the side, with four or five already near. A lesser animal would've been spooked by the nipping beasts, but Stardust's mettle was constant, his powerful legs sure. "Yah!" Renald cried, increasing the beats on his ribs, searching the painted tepees frontward for the sign of the red bear. Lodges whizzed by in a blur. An arrow whistled past him and stuck in the ground ahead, a moment later smashed by Stardust's hoof. Just one arrow? A second sailed by, then a third. But not ten, not twenty. These were cautious shots, not the torrent his mounted pursuers were capable of putting into the air, certain to bring him and his animal down. A mounted Comanche could discharge an arrow every two seconds with frightening accuracy, even by firing from beneath his horse's jaw. Hence their supremacy over other tribes, few of which were any good fighting from horseback. A dozen riders must be in range by now, with more and more joining the chase. At any moment they could end it if prepared to risk injury to their own people.

Eager to deny them a clean shot, Renald broke Stardust hard right, plunging into the village itself, forcing the tribespeople to jump back, spattering them with sand. "Move!" he yelled in Comanche. "Get inside!" As if charging ahead of a spring flood in a rocky wash, horse and rider negotiated the intervals between abodes, weaving left and right, while their pursuers coursed through behind them in a broad line.

To Renald the shelters seemed to rush forward like attackers he must dodge. About forty lodges deep into camp and three or four removed from the riverbed, a new chorus of yelps drew his attention toward the stream. There he saw a procession of riders, unhindered by obstacles, charging up and extending ahead of him. Its leader called back to the others, who repeated his cry down the line. Suddenly he veered toward Renald, followed by every second rider as they splintered off from the column.

To elude them, Renald kicked Stardust like an unloved beast. The precious sorrel, almost too regal for this kind of work, was soon hammering the ground with such determined force, swerving here and there, that Renald began to fear he would lose his footing. In fact, no sooner did the fear arise than somebody rolled an obstacle in their path—perhaps a drum—which Stardust ably bounded over but which tumbled riders caught unawares behind. Renald heard the neighs, thuds, snorts, and cries as horse after horse piled up, jettisoning their riders. He glanced back to see tepees collapsing in the massive slide of kicking bodies. With a smile of satisfaction he looked forward, where a distinct grouping of lodges appeared a hundred feet ahead to the left. Their buffalo-blood illustrations jumped out at him. Meantime, the flanking line of riders was spilling in from the same side, by now only one tepee distant. Veering left toward his target, he broke through the Comanche line, dropping a few riders, one thrown wildly into the wall of an abode, another hitting the dirt after a failed saddle-to-saddle bid to dislodge him. At last Renald found himself steps away from a stream-facing lodge whose backside bore the image of a bear.

He yanked Stardust to a breathless halt outside the flap door. Before it, a head-dressed elder in an embroidered white robe stepped back from the spray of coarse sand. Another ten seconds and Renald could've avoided the fight to come.

Just as he was pivoting to dismount he became conscious of an indistinct form rising in the air and arcing toward him. The shape was like that of a huge flying squirrel, limbs spreading, and behind it the shimmering mane of a horse, the sheen of its back. He stretched his focus. Now nearly upon him, the thing took the form of a man in flight. Fierce eyes registered, flailing ribbons of hair, sun-glinting shoulders. In a prolonged instant, the separate parts of man and beast formed wholes in Renald's mind, revealing a sequence of actions whose impact he now felt. He'd barely gotten his hands aloft before the body came crashing into him like a cannonball. To lessen the blow, Renald took it revolving off his saddle. Luckily his boot cleared the stirrup. Locked chest to chest, the two men went down like a cask off a wagon. They hit the ground rolling, a cloud of dust rising around them. When the swirl cleared, the breech-clothed brave was atop Renald's chest, pinning his arms, that long black hair falling in sheets around the Indian's face. In the gap between those falls, Renald writhed against the foul steam of his opponent's breath, wincing as sweat dripped like hot wax from the other's brow. It might've been over already, but the warrior bore no weapon. Pinned as he was, Renald could reach neither the gun at his hip nor the knife on his chest. Instead the brave went for Renald's blade with his teeth, plunging down and coming up with it, handle gritted. He pivoted his head for the downward slash.

A white column with a feathered plume to Renald, the old man stepped into view beside the brave and laid a hand on his shoulder, halting the action. The youth's chest palpitated violently. Only now was he winded by the fall. Above, the chief frowned, folds of skin fringing beady eyes that bore down on Renald.

From beneath the blade, Renald wheezed, "Pardon the intrusion, Chief."

Albeit a toothless one, a smile graced Red Bear's face. "Captain Renald! *Unha hakai nuusuka?*"—"How are you?"

"*Tsaaku, unse?*"—"All right, and you?"

The chief ordered the brave off. Falling back a step with a grunt, the warrior spit the dagger into the palm of his hand, then sucked air. Renald got to his feet, dusting himself. He unstrapped the knife belt and threw it against the youth, who clutched it to his heaving chest, baffled.

"If you like the taste of it ..." said Renald, "... have the rest!"

Still more diminutive but broad fighting men were halting their animals and leaping to the ground, some grasping bows, some knives, some guns, some just air. Having been ripped from slumber, most were insufficiently garbed, the bare-chested ones covered in goosebumps. Several put themselves between Renald and their chief before Red Bear implored them to disperse. From the quiver of a turning brave, Renald withdrew an arrow by the fletching. He broke it into an inverted *V* and threw it at Red Bear's feet.

The old chief righted himself to the extent he could. "That's the *Apache* sign of peace," he said. "You Apache?"

Renald found enough breath to laugh. He jutted a thumb over his shoulder toward the mob. "They know what it means." Then, "It's been many moons, Chief. If you are well I am glad."

"I am well. My family is well." Red Bear waited for an explanation.

Renald's brow furrowed. "Fact is, family is the reason for my visit. *My* family."

"Oh?" the chief exclaimed. He seemed surprised, but not surprised enough. Did he know something?

"Yeah," said Renald, locking Red Bear's guarded gaze. "Seems I got more family here in this village than anyplace else in Texas."

A mantled, spindly woman appeared from the darkness of Red Bear's lodge, and Renald pinched the brim of his hat. Frankly, he couldn't tell one wife from another. He remembered Iron Mountain once joking that Red Bear slept between his two wives, careful not to roll to one side or the other.

"I have something to show you, Chief," he continued. "You and Talking Moon."

Red Bear told his woman to prepare his pipe. "First we smoke together."

Renald grinned, feeling the stretch on his dry cheeks. In English he replied, "That sounds mighty fine."

To the throngs of men gathering around them, Red Bear said, "Send a rider to Talking Moon. Tell him Captain Renald has come to see him."

The nearest warriors traded bewildered glances. The chief smiled at Renald. "You may tie your animal at my tepee. My wives will prepare a meal."

"But his weapon!" objected one brave, pointing at Renald's sidearm as he bent down to secure Stardust.

The peace chief waved his hand dismissively. "He would be safer using it on himself than against us."

With that, he took Renald by the elbow into his tepee.

Part V
Taiboo Tekwa—
Talks White

Chapter Twelve

When Cole Hawker rendezvoused with 10th Troop they weren't singing Irish marching tunes but Negro spirituals. "How can yer captains march to this!" he protested, aligning his horse with Black Jack Davidson's at the head of the column.

"Maybe they'll sing 'Garryowen' next," Davidson replied from his saddle, glumly.

"That'll be the day!" This from "Tops" Chance, riding abreast.

The hide man could scarcely hear them over "Go Down Moses." Now late afternoon, he'd met the rearguard a half-day's ride from North Scalp. After showing the lieutenant his commission, two corporals galloped him up the creaky, lumbering pack train of buckboards and mules to the vanguard. With these agile means of transport, the 10th had facilely traversed North Scalp Gorge and then diverted northward to skirt the western edge of the Tonk Forest. There, a cadre of four Tonkawa scouts had joined the column, informing Davidson of Chief Buffalo Run's disappearance in pursuit of Renald. Receiving their orders, they promptly formed the advance with a trooper named Tyler. Among their tasks was to determine where to bivouac and the time required at marching speed from there to the Double Barrel. Trooper Tyler later doubled back to report the way clear to within telescopic sight of the rock itself, striking distance from the gorge, while the others rode on to survey its ridgelines and entry points. Perhaps they would even sight the enemy camp.

With Hawk and the topographical engineer, Wallace, on his left, his orderly riding behind, and Captain Norton on his right with Sergeant Chance, Davidson ordered Tops to signal walking rest. In his outfit, that meant quiet too. Chance dutifully raised his hand and called out the order. Behind them by unit the soldiers tugged rein on their black and brown chargers, stepping down only when a second command was called: *"Diiis-mouuunt!"*

As Hawk unburdened his mare, Chance leaned over to Davidson. "See what I mean?"

"About what, Tops?"

" 'Bout how he sags his horse. That there animal is bent in the middle."

"So it is," replied his superior, unamused. "I pity that animal."

The officers stepped down. Hawk came round his horse to lead from the right, putting him shoulder to shoulder with his commander.

Visibly disappointed his hunter had returned empty-handed, Davidson called through his whiskers for Hawk's report; but when Hawk began recounting events from the beginning, he cut him short. "Dictate the full report to my orderly when we pitch camp. Doubtless it'll make unsettling bedside reading. For the present I want to know three things—where's Laura Little, where's Scott Renald, and where the hell is Texas Tonk?"

Hawk shuddered, expelling air so trail-pungent it must've made Davidson long for his old whiskey breath. His view fell upon the wide open spaces ahead, the dusty rises and falls. "Texas is dead," he answered. "The woman is riding with Dead Meat now. When me and Renald parted ways, he was setting out fer the Quahada camp. I judged it prudent to swing back." Quite aware of how he sounded, the big man sheepishly met the colonel's glare.

"Mission abandoned," Davidson emphasized.

"You ought to know what yer marching into."

"What *we* are marching into. You're staying with us, Mr. Hawker."

Hawk swallowed. "I am?"

Davidson might've probed Texas' fate or Renald's second disappearance, but mention of the southern chief had duly arrested his interest. The presence of Penateka this far north was a major piece of intelligence. "Carne Muerto, you say?"

"Yessir. Seems the Penateka are combining with the Quahada. Dead Meat's leading an advance party of about twenty bucks to Talking Moon. Fearsomest-looking band you ever saw."

"Did he say where Talking Moon's encamped?"

"Damned if he didn't draw us a map!"

"I'm in no humor for sarcasm, Mr. Hawker. And don't think you can mock me because you're a civilian."

Hawk hooked a finger in his waist belt, his belly flopping out. "Surely didn't mean nuttin' by it, sir. It ain't Dead Meat's part of the country. Seemed he figured on riding the ravine straight through, eastward. Renald reckons they're hiding under that pedestal rock."

"We figure that too," said Engineer Wallace. "Makes for a meeting point."

"Just where did you encounter Chief Carne Muerto?" asked Colonel Davidson.

"Survivor's Bluff. You was right about Renald's route. I found him and the woman pinned down there by some Tonkaways. From the ridge, he'd emptied most of their saddles."

"What about Chief Buffalo Run?"

"Renald introduced him to the Great Spirit."

Davidson pinched his eyes shut, aghast. "So that's what happened. Tonkawa scouts told us of the chase."

"If I could offer an opinion, sir ..." said Hawk.

"You may."

"He done what he had to. Back in the basin we come across two bodies, Tonkaways that jumped him. One was Texas' own brother."

"Lordy-lordy," exclaimed Chance, one horse removed. "What about Texas? He was already gunning for Renald."

"She did him."

Davidson was stunned. "You're telling me the governor's niece shot down an army corporal in cold blood?"

"I ain't defending her, but it was a Comanche squaw done that. Way she sees it, she was *our* captive. Now them Penatekas got all 'em Henrys!"

Colonel Davidson responded with suitable irritation. "Those guns were meant as a deterrent against Comanche aggression, not to arm the Comanche against us."

Straightening himself under his commander's withering eye, Hawk answered, "They wasn't intended to be used against Scott Renald, neither. If you'll pardon the expression, sir, the whole thing's as mixed up as a shit hole. The Tonkaways shoulda stayed in their forest."

"I'll have you restrain your opinions from this point forward, Mr. Hawker!" Davidson growled. To Norton, he called, "Captain, isn't a government scout subject to military discipline?"

"Sure is!" came the reply.

Hawk turned imposingly, shoulders bulging under the hide he wore. "Just who you fixing on court martialing, Colonel? Renald or me?"

"And what about you?" Davidson fired back. "How is it I sent out a bear and got back a barn mouse?"

Hawk tensed from the neck up. "Now lookee who's being funny! Least I'm alive! Same is the woman. Same is Renald ... last I seen him, anyway. That's worth something, I reckon." He bobbed his head. "Ain't it? How 'bout a drink!"

Frowning, Davidson called for the sergeant's saddle flask. Receiving it under his horse's jaw, he passed it to Hawk, who was already licking his whiskers. The frontiersman unscrewed the cap and guzzled like one dying of thirst. In revulsion Davidson ripped the thing away. "And what about Renald?" he barked. "How come he disobeyed my orders and rode for the Comanche camp?"

"Pardon me, sir," offered Captain Norton, "but what did he have to lose at that point?"

Hawk ran his sleeve across his parched lips and wiry beard. "You'd be surprised! He's got everything to lose if we raid into the Quahada Comanche."

Davidson filled his lungs. "What the hell is that supposed to mean?"

"It means you ought rethink that court martial." The hide man grinned through his beard. "Sure you want the full report later? 'Cause I got some story fer you ..."

The yellows and reds of the landscape soon became oranges and violets in the failing light as dusk approached faster than their destination did. Tomorrow before sunup they would call "boots and saddles" and by first light probe the gorge as intelligence advised.

* * *

Some minutes after Chief Red Bear showed Renald inside his lodge, the drum of hoofbeats interrupted their pipe smoking. Ducking under the open flap, they emerged linked by the chief's hand tucked in a fatherly manner under the white man's jacket sleeve. By this time hundreds of warriors had massed between the tepees outside, both mounted and on foot, waiting for something to happen.

The venerable Red Bear's automatic embrace had established Renald's neutrality beyond a doubt, but the air was still thick with apprehension. Most of the men were Comanche, but Renald recognized some clusters as Kiowa and Arapahoe and others as Cheyenne dog soldiers. The latter, he guessed, were remnants of the fighters smashed by Colonel Carr up in Kansas at the Battle of Summit Creek, where Tall Bull had fallen. Their presence this far south, within Comanche ranks, was evidence both of their plight and of Talking Moon's powers of persuasion.

The hoof thunder ended somewhere out of sight. Within moments, amidst shouting from the back, those warriors closest to Renald made way for a force wedging through the crowd. In rode a headdressed, buckskin-clad figure on a powerful dapple grey. Around the animal's muscular neck hung a chain of scalps. Coup stick in hand, the rider maneuvered the beast in circles before Renald, spitting curses all the while. Renald let him get it out.

Next, perhaps out of respect for the elder chief, Talking Moon leapt from his horse and confronted the *taiboo* on foot.

Renald looked him up and down. His stature was impressive, but his years weren't.

From beneath his war bonnet's foot-high antlers, Talking Moon glared at Renald with equally blue eyes. He raised his knobby coup stick.

"Don't you dare," muttered Renald. "And let's dispense with the native invective. I know you talk white. Fact, I know your mother was a schoolteacher."

Opposite him, Talking Moon recoiled, slack-jawed. Then, gathering himself, he grasped the coup stick at both ends, muscles swelling under the buckskin, his eyes flaring.

"I've come to discuss the white boy you're holding," said Renald.

"White boy?" Talking Moon huffed. "Apache took two *taiboo* boys ... south of the Colorado."

"That's useful to know, but I don't mean the Hermanns. I mean your son."

Visibly horrified, the chief responded, "My son?"

"You're a half-blood, Chief. I see it in your face, your height. Nobody knew it till now. Nobody got close enough whose scalp you didn't take. But you must've feared this day would come."

Talking Moon laughed scornfully. "I fear nothing."

"Sure," said Renald.

The chief pursed his lips. Then, "Boy mama send you?"

"In a way, yes."

"She think he can live white? She think he *taiboo* now?" He uttered the word with obvious contempt.

"He's sure got a lot of white blood in him. Don't pretend you Comanche despise it. Why else did your father and you make white women your squaws?"

Talking Moon stepped forward, irritation intensifying. "You brave come here for man's son."

Renald dug into his shirt pocket and produced the portrait. At first the chief hesitated. Then he snapped it away. He laid eyes on Margaret Chase on her wedding day. His tone fell with his fading scowl. "I got no picture of her, no picture at all."

"You do now." Renald breathed in. "That's my sister you're looking at."

Talking Moon's eyes seemed to swell in their sockets. "What you said?"

"Your elders know me, their squaws welcome me with cooking. Yet those blue eyes of yours have seen me for the first time. Makes a man wonder why."

A silence followed during which the chief, color fading, seemed to grasp what was happening and to search Renald's face for family traits. An observer might've noted similarity in their high foreheads and jutting jaws. In his boots and hat, Renald stood only slightly taller. At last, Talking Moon said, "I heard about *taiboo* many time in Comanche country, trade with my father."

"Not only with him." Renald acknowledged Red Bear. "The chief here knows Iron Mountain kept you and your mother hidden from me, just told me so himself. On one occasion Iron Mountain short-ordered you down to Penateka country to get you gone quick. I saw your party riding away. You were small warrior then."

Talking Moon swelled his chest. "I am war chief now."

"You're still my nephew, like it or not."

He anticipated Renald's demand. "Small warrior should be with big warrior."

"So you can take him scalp hunting?" He shook his head. *"Boy mama left him."*

"That's not the way I heard it. And the papers that carry men's words reported she tried to come back. It broke her heart to lose that boy."

Talking Moon eyed him ferociously. "So what you want, to fight me for my son?" He slapped his own chest. "Come on."

Renald shook his head. "I don't have to fight you. I'm your blood elder."

The chief retreated a step, as if dealt a blow. He shook his stick in frustration. "But you not Comanche!"

"What's that to me? Your elders may be afraid to contest you, but your war policy is putting everybody's children at risk." He turned to his audience. "I am the brother of Margaret Renald Chase, known to you as She Rode West. As Talking Moon's uncle, I call a council fire on the arrival of Chief Carne Muerto of the Penateka."

A collective gasp sucked the air. The restless crowd spread his words rapidly.

Astonished, Talking Moon had parted his lips too. A long, tense pause followed. Then, with his free hand, he reached for his blade. But Renald had the draw on him. The chief froze with an inch of flint exposed. Around them, the close-in braves drew their blades. But Red Bear rivaled Talking Moon in authority there. In a cracking, high-pitched voice, the peace chief appealed for them to desist. He faced Renald.

"You cannot call an elder meeting," he scolded. "But I can."

Renald spun his six-shot into its holster and sized up his opponent. "You're a sorry sight—holding your mother's image in one hand and a knife meant for her brother in th'other."

Letting go of the blade, Talking Moon folded his arms and bounced on the heels of his moccasins. "Carne Muerto?"

"I met him on the Llano. He'll tell you I shot down a party of Tonkawa. Not that I'm looking for thanks."

"We heard about a Tonkawa war party," said Red Bear. "It was riding into nowhere."

"They had a purpose," replied Renald, his gaze settling on his nephew. "They were giving chase to me and your squaw."

"My squaw?" said Talking Moon.

"One of 'em." Renald sang the name with a hint of mockery. "*Watsi-ni Nuena*. Remember her? The blond?"

"We speak not her name," the chief grunted.

"You will again, I'm afraid. She insists on it. I reckon they'll reach here before sundown."

Talking Moon's youthful face was lined with anguish. "What you do with my wife?" He pointed south. "Out there."

"I rescued her from the Tonk after they massacred some agency breakouts. I reckon you know about that."

"You kill chief too?"

"I ain't proud of it," Renald responded. "Take me to the boy."

Sweat broke out on Talking Moon's brow. Circumstances had run roughshod over him. "Why I do that?" he protested.

Renald treated it like acquiescence. In Comanche he said, "Before Red Bear and your people, give me your word you will not strike me nor order me struck."

"No need," pronounced Red Bear. "I guarantee your safety. We will visit the boy together. But first a smoke in my lodge, the *three* of us." To no effect he called for the crowd to disperse.

Taking each man by the elbow, one more reluctant than the other, he led them into his tepee.

* * *

Talking Moon threw open the flap of Red Bear's hut and strode forward with princely comportment, his normal color restored under the feathered and horned headdress. Scott Renald followed him out, expressionless. Behind them came Red Bear wearing the last of a placating smile. In the hour gone by not one warrior had abandoned the place—all, thanks to the village women, were now protected against the morning chill by clothing or buffalo hides. Taking notice of his warriors, Talking Moon repeated the cry for their dispersal, but nobody was quick to regain his mount except himself, with Renald closely following suit. Red Bear raised a hand of parting as the men pushed their way through the bodies toward the riverbed and started eastward. By this time, the drama of the *taiboo*'s arrival had been retold to the last tepee, and all the inhabitants had come out of their dwellings, the din of their anxious exchanges forming a constant rumble in the natural vessel of the gorge. Having shared the pipe with Red Bear, the men rode abreast in silence to the edge of camp.

Reaching the last rows of tepees before the ravine walls converged to bracket the stream, just fifty yards apart, the chief dismounted and handed his reins to a waiting youth, his war bonnet to another. "Come!" he told Renald. As the awestruck crowd edged aside, Talking Moon and the white man stepped past several dwellings till a lodge emerged that had to be his. Ringing the circumference above the entryway was a painted black band a yard high. In it, a series of four illustrations depicted the lunar cycle, ending with the sacred circle in the form of a white-painted shield suspended above the doorway. Below stood two buffalo-robed women, squat and somber, one with her brown hands crossed over the chest of a blue-eyed, rosy-cheeked, fair-haired boy. Excepting the length of his locks and fringed clothing, he looked like a white child. Why shouldn't he? In store clothes he would pass for one. Be one?

Talking Moon stepped aside, and the boy lifted disquieted eyes to Renald, who rolled his shoulders uncomfortably.

The chief said, "My son. He is called Taiboo Tekwa—Talks White."

Renald slid his nephew a look. "Talking Moon, Whispering Wind, and now *Talks White*. You trying to say something?"

"Boy talk white make him different other boys." The chief prodded his son's shoulder. "You proud, no? Talk *taiboo* like father ..."

"Better than you!" The boy stepped out of the woman's grasp and approached the tall man. "My mother teach me. But she gone." He sounded—seemed—remarkably civilized. Yet this was a child who'd never known civilization. Renald remembered what Laura Little had said about teaching him to read and write in anticipation of the tribe's full domestication. And here was his sister's grandson, besides. Biting his lip, Renald struggled for words. Decades ago, at an officers' dance, he'd become similarly speechless before a major's daughter and her father in another life-altering moment. He eyed the child's father for a prompt. "Chief?"

Talking Moon cleared his throat and told his son, "This man Scott Renald. He brother of Grandma." *Grandma*. Renald marveled at the word coming from a Comanche.

The boy viewed him with widened eyes. That was all.

Renald dropped to his left knee, extending his gloved hands, upturned. When Taiboo Tekwa did not react, he cupped his shoulders instead. "Call me *uncle*. Do you know that word?"

The boy shook his head.

"*Un-cull.* Your grandma's brother. We are family."

The child showed no reaction, except to tremble perceptibly. Did he sense change? So much for Renald's efforts to avoid frightening him. Perhaps lowering himself to the boy's level—which no Comanche male would do—hadn't helped. Renald rose to his full height and gripped his belt buckle with both hands. In a monotone, he asked, "How old are you, young man?"

Taiboo Tekwa brightened. "I am six springs old—and one summer!"

"You don't say! Why, you'll be going on your first hunt soon enough. And what sorts of things do you like to do?"

After first glancing at his father, the boy answered, "I like to chase prairie dog. I like to run along the stream with my friends when my father say it okay. I like to watch the men come home."

Renald nodded. "Today, I expect, somebody else is coming home—to you." He tipped his hat toward Talking Moon. "You tell him, Chief."

In their language, father told son.

Taiboo Tekwa's eyelids fluttered in wonder.

Renald said, "She's coming back to hold you close."

With pale disbelief the boy sought his father's confirmation. But Talking Moon was stone-faced. Turning back to Renald, Taiboo Tekwa's expression seemed to waver between joy and fear. It was hard telling. The chief glanced uncomfortably at his other wives, both of whom looked downhearted. They seemed to understand. At last he told his son, "She ride with chief from south. This man …"—he seemed to peel the name off his tongue—"… Uncle Scott … he say she come tonight."

Before his son could smile, he added, "She not stay long."

Renald shook his head at Talking Moon. "She loves you," he told the boy, "as only a mother can."

The child teared up. He retreated shoulder-first into the sheltering arms of the woman behind him. Renald began yanking the gauntlet of his glove nervously.

Talking Moon ended the meeting. He gestured toward the perimeter. "You and me talk there."

Before the women pulled the boy into their hut, Renald gave him a final smile, all teeth and chin.

* * *

Scrutinizing the ravine's lofty *V,* Renald began to think like the officer he had been. Situated just before the bend leading to its mouth, this part of the gorge was probably as secure and defensible a waterside position as could be found anywhere in the remote hideaways of dry country. However, in these confined quarters the Comanche couldn't form long offensive lines to outflank a troop and ring its defensive circle. Only scattered bunches could mount an attack on a penetrating force, mere target practice for dismounted soldiers squinting down the sights of their Springfields. Nevertheless, the Springfields were single-shot and prone to jamming, whereas the mounted fighters could attack in wave after wave, never ceasing their volleys of arrows as their counterparts stationed on the walls engaged in a vicious crossfire ambush. He pondered the impact of Carne

Muerto's repeaters on the outcome. Yet Renald trusted in Davidson's forbearance not to enter the gorge alone. More likely, the lieutenant colonel would plug the exit and wait for the stronger regiments to arrive. Where the ground allowed, the other troops would spill down the walls, and, together with Davidson's 10th, squeeze the survivors into submission.

"I stay here with my best fighters and young ones who need to fight," said the proud chief, his vast camp outstretched behind him. "Each brave know his position in rocks." He pointed here and there. "We got some repeaters. I post men with mirrors from start of gorge. You see, we learn something from Yellow Stripes."

"You sure have," Renald responded. "My compliments on your location and camp layout. It's invisible to scouts atop the southern ridge, and ..."—he jabbed his finger ahead—"... if soldiers penetrate beyond that bend there, *pow!*" Against a single, westward marching battalion led by a careless commander, Talking Moon's position was very strong indeed. Against the inconceivable—in fact, the inevitable—it was very weak.

The war chief glowed with pride. "You worry, Uncle?"

"I'm a little worried."

"You should be. Men march from Fort Sill to here."

So he knew that much. It explained the absence of rearguard sentries. He had forward scouts tracking Davidson. "Doesn't mean they know your location," Renald replied, unconvincingly.

"I not stupid, Captain. You know we here. They know we here."

Renald studied the other's glib look. "It won't be pretty for either side, Chief. They'll lose some getting in, but ..."—he thumbed backward over his shoulder—"... you're burdened by all those women and children."

The chief replied in his own language. "They will be ready."

Should the unlikely happen, Talking Moon expected simply to slip his village out the back way, or ways. Because Sheridan's sweep had no prior precedent—never had columns marched from the south—the chief couldn't guess that thousands of men were, in fact, converging on his hiding place from every direction. The greatest danger was from the pony herd. A stampede would level the camp and do the army's work indiscriminately. The way Renald saw it, only he could prevent this happening. But to protect the women and children he must aid and abet the enemy. He dipped his gaze as if to an imaginary line and thought it over. The worse treachery, he decided, was to stand back and do nothing—nothing to stop a potential ambush of the cavalry and nothing to stop a raid on the village. As if edging the point of his boot across a real border, he cautioned, "Shouldn't you put that plan into action right now?"

Talking Moon's chest rose under the fringed buckskin. "Comanche, Kiowa, Cheyenne not run forever. From this ground we stop Yellow Stripes—together. Then we demand Palo Duro and north to old Camp Nichols."

These lands and the Neutral Strip. So that was it. A second reserve, but one on good land, sacred land, independent of fort control.

"You suppose the government will reward you for a massacre of its troops?" Renald lowered his voice but spit out his words with impatience. "What'd you get for Adobe Walls but more fighting, more incursions? There ain't enough buffalo left to last you through the winter. You'll get better by offering peace. If you answer Davidson with lead and arrowheads instead, many of your people will die. Picture the survivors on the long walk across the desert with just the clothes on their backs. Picture it, because you won't be there to see it. You'll be conveniently dead. When Bad Eagle and Wild Horse rode their bands in to Sill, they pulled a train of their possessions behind them. The Quahada are about to lose everything, thanks to *you*."

Talking Moon crossed his arms over his thick chest. "You talk but not convince."

Renald searched his nephew's familiar eyes. "Didn't think I would. Just let me ride out the same way I came in, but with the boy. If the army already knows this position you've nothing to fear from me."

The war chief smiled, somewhat subversively. "You know camp layout. You alive only because we family."

"Let me keep your boy alive," said Renald.

"He not want to ride with you."

"He'll do like you tell him. His mother will ride with us too."

"Ah! You get my son *and* my woman!"

"I don't see it that way."

The chief shifted his weight. "I die, what happen to him?"

"Same that'll happen if you live. Maybe *that's* why you keep fighting, Chief. You surrender, you lose him."

Talking Moon stiffened. "Mount your horse. You ride to Red Bear. When Carne Muerto come, I come." With that, he turned toward the camp and began barking orders at his men.

Chapter Thirteen

By the time Renald returned to Red Bear's tepee, under the watch of a single brave, the air had warmed with the rising sun and the village was full of activity. While fighting-age men were making arrows and equipping their mounts, the women were minding their children and weaving in groups. This was normal to witness in an Indian camp. Yet a number of absences had struck Renald from atop Stardust, the first being that of sound. Something close to silence prevailed in a village that might've been clamorous with boys and girls at play, the washboarding of clothing, and the scraping and beating of hides. Renald also noticed that nobody went near the stream, even to fetch water. Travoises were now standing idle everywhere, some fitted with dangling dog harnesses, as if the tribe could really outrun the cavalry while pulling its stuff. What a way for a people to live—in perpetual fear; and what a way for children to be brought up, feeling hunted. Here among the untamed Comanche the situation was even bleaker than on the reservation, and, to a reasonable man, utterly hopeless.

When he reentered Red Bear's lodge, he noted the absence of
the utensils, medicine bag, and the decorative arms he'd seen
strung up along the interior walls earlier. Stuffed parfleches
now lay like slumbering dogs around the inner edge. Red Bear
was ready to run too.

Renald found him and his eldest wife sitting by a small cook
fire in the center of the room. She was stirring a pot of stew, the
air heavy and redolent of spices. His stomach seemed to turn
inward on itself, reminding him he could eat. Here, at home,
the peace chief was not wearing his headdress—it sat handily
atop one of the large, folded bags. Both husband and wife
wore their hair parted in the middle and over their shoulders.
In Renald's absence she had added colorful beaded necklaces
to her appearance. Her walnut face cracked into wrinkles as
she welcomed him with a smile.

He gestured toward the nearest sack. "Going somewhere?"

Red Bear beckoned him to join them. "Today a patrol is near."

Renald folded his legs beside Red Bear and replied in the
chief's language. "It is more than a patrol."

"Pony soldiers do not enter ravines. Perhaps they will ride
past."

"Maybe. But the day of change is coming. It's coming on a ..."
He made the hand signs for a fast horse.

Red Bear nodded, sadly. "We all know it."

"Now—*right now*—is your chance to keep what is yours or
lose everything. This I told Talking Moon."

The chief and his wife traded looks. "But it made no
difference," the old man ventured. His wife served their guest
a steaming tin bowl, army-issue, and a spoon ground from
elk bone. Contrary to the last time he'd been offered stew, on
this occasion Renald could be sure it didn't contain chunks

of man. It struck him that, though the camp was replete with white man's stuff, acquired in trade or raid, its inhabitants all seemed to defy the native tendency nowadays to dress halfway this and that. By design?

For a while they ate their meal in silence. Finally Renald raised a question. "What follows after you leave your tepees behind? That's too much weight to pull and get away. The way I see it, you can replace them only by trading your horse wealth with the Cheyenne." He put down his spoon. In English complemented by hand signals, he said, "That'll lead to more raiding and more punitive action by the cavalry."

"We know that too," answered the chief.

"If you surrender you can pull your tepees behind you." Renald spread his hands wide. "You can have all this somewhere else."

"We talk of it," admitted Red Bear. He gestured toward the entryway. "But we say it behind their backs. They threaten those who would leave."

"Talking Moon threatens? You?"

Red Bear spit over his shoulder. "That is what has joined him from the reservations. The worst." He thumbed his chest. "At heart, the son of Iron Mountain is his father's son ..."

"That is not what I heard."

Shaking his head of white hair, the chief said, "There would be challenges to his authority if he did not push his policy to the end. For a war chief, taking the fight to the enemy is a form of defense."

"Not when it is against settlers, buffalo hunters."

"That is not how they see it."

"I know how they see it, Chief. But it is raids against settlers and hunters that bring the troops, that bring the day of change forward."

Lowering his eyes, the chief answered, "Every time a new party joins us, my sadness grows, but I am powerless to stop the raiding. His men burn like timber. They are many, and they are strong."

"What good will their fire be in the winter? The buffalo is in the lands of the Arapahoe and Cheyenne."

"You speak the truth," said Red Bear. "The herds in the Palo Duro are not sufficient anymore. The Southern Cheyenne claim there are many buffalo north of us, beyond the lands between."

"The Neutral Strip," said Renald in English.

"But many forts stand there too. Even Cheyenne dog soldiers have sought shelter with us." Red Bear passed his empty bowl to his wife.

Renald followed his lead, exclaiming, "Tasty!"

Cheeks rising with delight, she gestured toward the buffalo-paunch pot.

Renald declined with a smile. Then to Red Bear, "As delicious as it is, it's small game. *Tabukina?* Back in Indian Territory, Chiefs Bad Eagle and Wild Horse are afraid you will all starve come winter. This message I will deliver to the elders."

"We will listen. But if I know Talking Moon, we will surrender only because of starvation or defeat."

"What about the boy?"

For a moment Red Bear hid his eyes beneath folds of skin. "I will speak on the boy's behalf and advise that you be made his guardian in the event of war. But you will be stripped of your horse and your weapons and confined to a tepee."

"I proposed to Talking Moon I take the boy and his mother out, same way I came in."

"The council will not approve that. It would start a panic."

Renald was about to reply when the flap door opened with a snap. There was Talking Moon's rigid frame filling the breach. His impassive face suggested he'd overheard something of the discussion. An awkward moment passed for the men seated. Ducking his head inside, the war chief appraised the stripped-down interior approvingly before addressing Renald. "My son want 'Uncle Scott.' "

Renald and Red Bear exchanged looks.

"He may enter," replied the peace chief, hand outstretched.

Eyes fixed on Renald, Taiboo Tekwa slipped past his father. He was holding the photograph of Margaret Chase.

"I return soon," Talking Moon told Renald. In Comanche, "Do not speak of things he does not need to know." He frowned and was gone.

Sitting down cross-legged beside Renald, Taiboo Tekwa looked back and forth between the image in his hands and the white man.

"Think we look like brother and sister?" asked Renald.

The child nodded.

"We all have the same eyes, don't we?"

Red Bear's wife offered the boy food. When he confessed thirst, she fumbled around behind her and produced a skin bulging with water. Taiboo Tekwa grabbed it and downed some before thrusting it back.

"So …" Renald adjusted himself on the floor mat. "Just what would you like to talk about with your Uncle Scott?"

The boy said, "My mother."

First eyeing Red Bear, Renald replied, "You'll soon be able to talk to her yourself."

"If she come at night I will be asleep."

"There's tomorrow …" But would there be? Dawn was raiding time.

"Uncle Renald, where did she live in the white man's lands?"

"In a city called Fort Worth."

"What is a *see-teey*?"

"Oh, it's a big place," Renald answered with storytelling emphasis. "That is, it can grow big. They're just getting started in Fort Worth. We call it a cowtown. You see, cattle came in behind the buffalo in those parts. People live and work there, and boys and girls learn in buildings made of wood and stone. Fort Worth sits on a river called the Trinity. There are places where children play, men talk, and where women make themselves beautiful."

"My mother is beautiful!"

"Your mother is very beautiful."

"Uncle Scott, why did she want to live there?"

The line of inquiry was inevitable. Red Bear observed Renald cautiously. The white man breathed in. "Tell you what, let's ask her together. Say, I've got a good idea! Why don't you and me play a game. You want to play a game in English with your Uncle Scott?"

"Yessss!" the boy cooed. "I played games in English with my mother and with my grandmother."

Renald turned to their host. "May we, Chief …?"

Approving with a wave of his hand, Red Bear reclined on a stuffed hide to watch.

"Okay, then. Ever play 'Guess the Animal'?"

Lighting up, "I play that with my father!"

Leaning in, Renald said, "I bet you're pretty good."

"Very good!"

"Of course you are. But I reckon you don't know all the names in English."

His legs still crossed, Taiboo Tekwa grasped both knees. "I try!"

"Close your eyes then," Renald told him. "Now open your ears for a night creature. 'Hooh-hooh ... hooh-hooh!' "

"Owl!" cried the child.

"Very good! That was an easy one, though."

"For *me* it was!"

"Here comes another. This one has a big appetite. That means he eats a lot. 'Cluck-cluck-cluck ... cluck-clu—' "

Popping his eyes open, the boy exclaimed, "Turkey!"

"Right again! You sure can name a lot of animals in English. I bet Chief Red Bear didn't know that one!"

Red Bear understood enough to laugh.

"Let's try another one. Close 'em ..."

Taiboo Tekwa squeezed his eyes shut, and Renald made a deep-chested snorting sound. When the boy didn't identify it immediately, he added a hint by drumming the ground with his knuckles.

"Horse!"

"Nawwwww," moaned Renald.

"Cat!"

"You mean a mountain lion? Nawwwww. I bet Red Bear knows this one, but *no* telling, Chief!" To the boy, "Give up?"

Taiboo Tekwa slapped his thighs. "I don't know it!"

"You sure?"

Opening his eyes, he conceded, "I sure."

"Why, that's a *buffalo,* young man!"

The child tilted his head to one side. "I seen buffalo when I was three. But I don't remember. My father say the buffalo come back when the *taiboo nuu* go."

"Yes, I say that!" Talking Moon had reappeared in the doorway. Bending his knees, he stepped inside. He stood tall again. "Buffalo survive winter no problem. Not white man's cattle. This big problem for Fort Worth, I hear, and for agency Indian."

As Talking Moon had addressed his words to Renald, the *taiboo* responded. "Last winter was a hard one. But you prize cattle as much as the ranchers do. That's why you let the ranchers live, for a price."

"It smart business," said the chief. Lightening his tone, he continued, "You make sounds of animals good, Captain. Maybe you hunt with us. You wear *fox* skin." To his son, "You like your uncle?"

The boy jerked his head up and down.

"Think he funny?"

"He very funny, Father. He make animal sounds good as Comanche."

"Then we give him name," said the chief. "Talks Animal."

They all chuckled.

Talking Moon erased his smile and reached out, speaking in his own tongue. "Come, my son. Enough of your funny uncle." To Renald, he added humorlessly, "We meet at council fire."

The boy rose, protesting. His father was first out the door, dragging him by the arm. Framed in the doorway, Taiboo Tekwa twisted back, still holding the picture. "Uncle Scott, will my mother tell me a bedtime story?"

"Well, I don't know, son."

"Will you, Uncle Scott?"

Renald was spared a response by the boy's father, who tugged him away.

* * *

Renald was lashing a pile of sacks to a travois outside Red Bear's tepee when an easterly wave of commotion reached the village center. Like a chain of fire, word was spreading that a large band of Penateka Comanche armed with repeaters had arrived, and riding with them was Talking Moon's missing wife, Whispering Wind. With the guard assigned to Renald mounted opposite, he could do no more than watch the dense mass of villagers, whole families as well as fighting men, sweeping toward the corral in excitement—as though twenty guns could make the difference.

Only if Davidson was rash could they.

He must get to Carne Muerto before Talking Moon did. Picketed beside Red Bear's tepee, the crowd coursing around him, was Stardust, jerking his head and doing a nervous tap dance with his hooves. Across the way, Renald's mounted guard was trying to control his own agitated horse. Renald succeeded at making eye contact with the brave over the press of bodies. Indecision marked the young man's face. Surely he wanted to be the first to bring the news to his boss. Renald had an idea. "Go tell your chief!" he called. "Twenty guns!"

The warrior did not react.

Nevertheless, Renald was convinced he could be tipped. Over the din, he emphasized, "It's Carne Muerto! Don't let your chief be the last to meet him."

That was enough for the brave. He swung his horse around and rode off. Just then, Red Bear, fitting into his peace bonnet with both hands, came out of his hut to see Renald unclipping Stardust's lariat from the picket pin.

"I'll bring them here!" Renald cried, climbing into the saddle. Rousing Stardust with his heels, he guided him toward the vacant stream bed, the express path to Carne Muerto. A minute's gallop brought him to a clot in the sea of bodies, over his left shoulder, where those gravitating toward the newcomers met those following them. Standing in his stirrups, he scanned for the Penateka party between soaring tepees and over rounded, grassy wikiups, trying to single out the band and the woman who rode with it in the mass of clamoring heads, shoulders, and horses. Finally, where the crowd was thickest, the magnetic radiance of fair hair set aflame in the sun's last blast caught his eye. Sitting erect on her animal, she wore her hat behind her head, and from what he could tell at this distance was greeting her admirers with a warmth never witnessed on his watch, all smiles and nodding. He nosed Stardust closer, his attention, alas, arrested by those turquoise eyes, now embedded in a wildly sun-browned face. The crowd made way for him, a sign of the prestige he'd won standing up to Talking Moon.

Laura Little saw him first. She frowned. "I should've known …"

"You are unstoppable, Captain Renald," said Carne Muerto.

Tipping his hat, he replied, "I did offer to guide you. Got that horse under control?"

Dead Meat smirked beneath his headdress. "I think so."

Renald returned his attention to Laura Little astride the chief's light roan. Her hair fell in tangled curls over her tattered blouse, whose fringes rested on the thighs of her riding pants. Somehow, though her clothing was practically in ribbons, she had never seemed more collected. She'd never looked more attractive, either. Despite everything he'd gone through with her, despite his disappointment in her, he found himself stirred.

She leaned forward on her mount. "Just what're you doing here, Scott?"

Guiltily, he replied, "I wanted to control the outcome—what else?"

"You can't let go of the officer in you, can you?"

"I can't let go of a lot of things, Laura."

She straightened herself. "I told you, I'm Watsi-ni Nuena."

"For a day." He regarded Carne Muerto. "Chief, 10th Troop knows our location, and Talking Moon is positioning to ambush them inside the gorge."

"We saw dust to the west," replied Carne Muerto. "And to the south."

"The sweep," said Laura Little.

"So you told him," replied Renald, unsurprised. "I suggest we ride straight to the peace chief's lodge."

Carne Muerto sat himself taller—in Texas' saddle. "Talking Moon invited me, not Red Bear."

"You said you were coming to listen," replied Renald. "I urge you to start by listening to me, in private."

"I said I come to talk, not listen to a Yellow Stripe captain."

"Retired," Renald pointed out congenially.

After a pause Dead Meat said, "Okay. Show us the way."

Relieved, Renald reversed Stardust and swung him toward the stream, holding him back till the chief was riding abreast. Laura Little maintained her position at Carne Muerto's left. The Penateka warriors followed.

"What about my son?" she called to Renald.

"Wait your turn," he replied with annoyance. Then, to Carne Muerto, "Chief, if Talking Moon gets his hands on those repeaters you're carrying, he'll begin by baiting the regiment from Fort Sill. There'll be hell to pay."

"Hell?" replied Dead Meat. "We cannot keep the extras for ourselves. And I have not come to protest Talking Moon's judgment."

"You don't need to. I've already done it."

"*You?*" He laughed as if it were a joke.

Increasing the chief's amazement, Renald added, "I've called a council fire."

Carne Muerto's lips parted in astonishment.

Laura Little spoke for him. "*You* called a council? How'd my husband let you do that?"

Renald halted Stardust parallel to Red Bear's lodge, some three tepees in. The others followed his lead, and he nudged Stardust out to face them. Looking from Carne Muerto to Laura Little, he confessed, "I'm his uncle."

They both formed the sort of tight-lipped smile that follows a bad joke.

Renald continued. "I realized it, Laura, when you identified my sister in that photograph."

Carne Muerto passed her a look of surprise as hers became one of disbelief.

"Your sister?" Her voice betrayed no emotion. "You said nothing."

"I wanted to."

She shook her head. "Your eyes. I always felt there was something there."

"You've got a precious child, Laura," he said.

Hoof thumping erupted to the east. Leaving her sympathetic gaze, Renald reined Stardust around. Several riders were bearing down on them, one headdressed. As everybody's attention was seized by the thunder, he could feel the collective expectation of husband and wife's reunion, and the promise of chief joining chief in the common cause. He swallowed, dryly, unable to foresee the outcome of anything. Somehow, he must keep developments within his influence by making himself essential to any dialogue, any happening. All at once, Talking Moon was tugging back in a cloud of sand, his men forming a line at his rear. He gave Carne Muerto a cursory nod before confronting his wife with a hostility unexperienced even by Renald that morning. Without uttering a word he drove his mount against hers, forcing it back a few steps in whinnying protest.

"That is *my* horse she is riding!" Carne Muerto snapped.

With that, each band of warriors closed ranks around their leader while Talking Moon ordered his wife to dismount. Heedless of the greater confrontation he was provoking, he leapt from his animal brandishing his coup stick, jaw muscles working behind taut skin. He lurched forward, causing her to blink and brace for a strike; but like a wildcat he recoiled with a hiss, grinding the stick in his hands.

Renald slipped from his saddle. "Take it easy there, Nephew."

"I tell you stop, Talking Moon!" It was Red Bear's voice.

Renald slung his attention over his right shoulder to see the white-clad elder stepping out of the crowd. Then, reverting his focus, he saw that the peace chief's protestation had failed to influence. Sidestepping around her like a panther, Talking Moon berated his wife with a string of curses while she characteristically held her head high. If she were less proud, thought Renald, her husband might moderate his words, but now he was speaking as much to his audience as to her. Halting before her, he rose to his full height and censured her for all to hear. "Wife of Talking Moon wears white man's clothes!" He thrust the stick in Renald's direction. "Wife spends nights with other man!"

"Days too," she responded in English. "I hope you thanked him for it."

Then, with almost imperceptible speed, he wheeled around and swung the stick against her skull. She went down as

Renald sprang instantly to her defense, but, faster than the bow-twangs reached his ears, a bed of arrows appeared at his feet, and he toppled forward over them. He broke his fall with his hands and glanced right to see the mounted Quahada warriors reaching behind their shoulders to reload. He got to one knee to observe Talking Moon stalking his squirming victim, her face buried in the sand, a gash behind the ear turning her into a redhead. She'd taken the blow without even a whimper. As always, Renald found something to admire in her grit. But could she take another? He rose, fingers twitching.

Carne Muerto halted him. "This is not Fort Worth," he said.

"So we do nothing?"

Under his breath, Carne Muerto replied, "Let him weaken himself."

Renald's blood boiled. How far would Talking Moon take the chastisement? Laura Little's resolve could get her dead, or worse.

Talking Moon grabbed a fistful of her hair and bent her back like a bow, hissing in her ear, "Let the whole village know Whispering Wind is no longer wife of Talking Moon." He turned about and began to drag her by the hair downstream. She clawed his wrists from behind, screaming Comanche invective. His mounted men reversed and divided to give him space. The villagers, following, pressed as a group onto the stream bed. Leading Stardust forward alongside the Penateka line, Renald appealed to Carne Muerto for a sign. The chief cautioned, "She knew she must fight for her son."

"All it takes is one bullet," said Renald suggestively.

"But he's your nephew!"

"The white man has a saying, 'You don't choose your relatives.'"

Just then a shot rang out, and Talking Moon crumpled to the ground. The sudden roar through the peaceful gorge sent the warriors' horses into a frenzy, and both the Quahada and Penateka fought to hold their mounts. Even Stardust reared, before Renald jerked him down.

Where Talking Moon had fallen Laura Little rose, pistol in hand. Before all, she commenced driving the point of her boot into his gut, her hair consuming her face like a cluster of sagebrush. Kicking him again and again, she yelled, "I-want-to-see-my-son!" At last she left his body writhing in the dust and stamped his coup stick in two.

She turned full around, lifting a tattered shirttail and tucking the Colt under her belt. Striding forward to reclaim her mount, she passed Renald with a nod. He quipped, "You running for war chief?" Behind her, Talking Moon struggled to his feet but simply stood there, bent and faint, his antlered war bonnet tipped comically to one side and dark spots expanding in the buckskin below his shoulder, front and back. As Carne Muerto's riders promptly formed a defensive line around her, repeaters at the ready, Talking Moon's slack-jawed braves sat perplexed on their mounts. Were they to acknowledge their leader's defeat by standing down? Or were they to confront the Penateka? On their feisty mounts, they awaited Talking Moon's signal. Glaring after Laura Little, stricken with pain, he gripped his abdomen in one hand, his shoulder with the other, till he was cajoled away by women offering help. His men were absorbed into the crowd.

From atop the pale horse Laura Little thanked Carne Muerto for letting her do it.

Renald mounted up, then extended his open hand to her. "Best surrender that hog's leg."

Carne Muerto said, "Do it."

Frowning, she returned the gun to Renald, who slipped it under his belt. She reached up to her wound. Her hand came away coated.

Renald leaned over in his stirrup and had a look. "Don't you fret. That's a damn hard bone back there." Her hair was absorbing most of the bleed. When he leaned back to face her, a smile played on his lips. "After the squaws treat that, I'd be obliged to escort you to your son. He's expecting a bedtime story."

Brushing hair from her face, she said, "I'd kiss you—"

"Better not," he replied.

She sighed, drawing her horse toward an assemblage of waiting women.

Chapter Fourteen

The shot was detected by scouts from both Davidson's and Major Price's regiments. While the 10th was bivouacked east of the gorge, the major's 8th Troop was probing it from the west. When Davidson received the intelligence from his forward Tonkawa scouts, practically pinpointing the shot's origin at Double Barrel Rock, it was confirmation enough for him. He immediately dispatched riders to the other commanders. Two of Colonel Mackenzie's three columns were far distant, marching north from central Texas at thirty-mile intervals in their mop-up operations, but the colonel's 4th Cavalry and his colleague Colonel Buell, leading the 11th Infantry, were relatively close. Their proximity led Davidson to believe that sufficient force could be mustered at the gorge by sunup. With Price plugging the western exit, Mackenzie and Buell barring a southern escape, and Colonel Miles' 6th Troop arriving from Kansas to secure the northern ridge, the village would be hopelessly surrounded.

* * *

While Laura Little was being attended to by her helpers, about a dozen elders—including Kiowa and Southern Cheyenne chiefs—were meeting in Red Bear's lodge. Smoldering like a cast-out ember from the fire around which they sat, Talking Moon, his wounds dressed with tree moss, his gut wrapped and his arm slung, was propped on a bed of stuffed hides opposite Renald and flanked by Carne Muerto and Red Bear. After consuming a bottle of whiskey against the pain, the wounded chief had obstinately refused to be returned by travois to his tepee, insisting on being there.

At Renald's request, Carne Muerto brought the coffee and kettle he'd gained on Survivor's Bluff with his confiscation of the mule. Here, Renald made friends by cooking up a pot and pouring cups for all—all, that is, except Talking Moon, who rejected his in a snit. The calumet was passed around. Following some small talk and jovial back and forth, Red Bear opened the council by asking Carne Muerto to report what he'd seen on the Llano. Word about the dust clouds to the south and west had already circulated, however, and the men came with formed opinions about what to do. Red Bear led the faction wanting dialogue. "We can negotiate and see what terms we get," he said.

"Terms?" Talking Moon passionately roused himself from his drink-induced languor. "The first thing we lose when we lead our village in to Fort Sill is our horses. Without a horse, what is a Comanche? He cannot hunt. He cannot fight. He cannot teach his son bravery."

"What will we do with ourselves?" the Kiowa chief protested. "Weave with the women?"

"We must fight!" Talking Moon emphasized.

Glancing at Renald, Carne Muerto said, "I suggest we listen."

Talking Moon did not have much power to argue, or much influence suddenly. He'd lost face; besides that, his supposedly invulnerable person had been shot straight through. There was much animated discussion as the chiefs weighed the risks of either attacking the soldiers or attempting escape. Finally, a wait-and-see policy was adopted. This got Talking Moon muttering to himself in the smoky enclosure. More, it was decided that, although he would keep his war bonnet, a battle-fit warrior should assume temporary command as war chief. Healthy, experienced, and trilingual, Carne Muerto was the obvious choice. His twenty-plus repeaters factored in as well. To his nomination, Talking Moon gave the slightest nod of grudging approval.

Red Bear then spoke concerning the safety of Taiboo Tekwa and the custody issues. It was agreed that Whispering Wind's son would remain in his father's custody—after all, a boy belongs with his father—but Renald would be charged with his well-being in camp in the event of hostilities. On this matter, only the Quahada voted. Upon its approval Renald tried to offer Talking Moon a conciliatory look over the fitful flames, but his nephew's eyelids were shuttering down from drink and exhaustion.

As for accommodations, tepees for both Renald and Whispering Wind would be made available next to Red Bear's, whereas Carne Muerto and his men would billet near Talking Moon's lodge—a more strategic location, given what was known rather than suspected of the troop movements. Before bringing the meeting to a close, Red Bear and the Quahada elders together acknowledged Renald's service in delivering Whispering Wind into Carne Muerto's hands, and it was further agreed that Renald should keep his horse and weapons and move freely throughout the village without guard.

Finally, the peace chief told the *taiboo,* "The boy's father and I have witnessed his instant affection for you. Therefore, I ask the Quahada elders to approve you reuniting mother and son. You should have the satisfaction of witnessing it. The boy is waiting." The elders agreed with nods and grunts. "But," added Red Bear, "after that you turn your back. Henceforth you shall have no contact with another man's wife outside his presence."

"Did I misunderstand?" said Renald with the aid of signs. "I thought he just divorced her."

Red Bear placed a hand on Talking Moon's thigh. The chief was snoring. "He spoke in haste. It cannot be done in a fit of temper. Tonight he will rest here. Perhaps tomorrow we will discuss his marriage."

"Perhaps," said Renald.

* * *

It was twilight when Renald led his mount and hers to the lodge in which the village women were pampering her. The camp was remarkably quiet, calmed. He stepped near the door flap. "Laura?" Though he detected movement inside, voices, there came no immediate response. He cleared his throat. Feeling foolish, he tried, "Watsi-ni Nuena?" Then out she stepped, transformed. Her hair was clean and braided and tied back over her patched wound. Beneath an ornamented brown bison mantle she wore a beaded, white buckskin dress. Fitted to her neck was an inch-high ring of white beads, while resting on her bosom were several colorful stone necklaces. Her moccasins glittered with something. The village women had dressed her in their finest.

As for him, he wore his hat on his back, exposing his feathery hair above a toasted brow ribbed with deep lines.

"Well look at you," he said.

"Look at *you*," she replied. "How is it you always appear able, Captain Renald?"

"Rest," he answered halfheartedly. "Some men fasten thorns around their necks to keep awake in dangerous country. I just nod off." Then, "How's the head?"

"Worth it," she replied.

This time he didn't offer her help getting atop her mount, careful to avoid appearing too chivalrous with another man's property. She vaulted expertly onto the blanket anyway. He stepped into his saddle and chirruped Stardust forward. Glancing at the loaded sleds they were passing, she said, "You know, I'm glad to see the camp packed up. They'll have the night to accept the idea they'll be pulling those things into Fort Sill."

"Yeah. Instead of dragging 'em to yet another hiding place."

She held him in her view. "You actually softened his resolve."

"You call that soft? He sure swings a stick."

Gently, she patted the back of her head. "He was lashing out in frustration, like a child."

"In the end, you'll have saved the village and maybe some soldiers' lives. Tell me, did you work it out with Carne Muerto on the ride in? Or before that? You sure wanted a gun."

She smiled. "Wouldn't you like to know."

His eyebrows settled low. "You confound me, Laura. I *never* know what you'll do next."

"Yes, you do," she said. "I'm going to crush my boy with love."

Renald dipped his chin. "There he is ..."

A cry shattered the hush. *"Pia, nu Pia!"*—"Mother, my mother!" From between the lines of tepees ahead came the blur of a little figure, arms outstretched. Laura Little slipped from her mount to receive the impact of Taiboo Tekwa's tearful embrace. They shared joyful sobs, exchanged loving words. After a while she turned her wet cheek and lifted glassy, fluttering eyes to Renald.

He responded with a fleeting smile before cutting the air with the single-fingered salute he reserved for women. Then he reined Stardust around and rode away.

* * *

The common anxiety in the village made it a sleepless night for most, excepting Scott Renald, of course. As was universally anticipated, when the veils of mist had all but vanished, and Double Barrel Gorge was struck by sunbeams and arched with faint rainbows, word spread westward from its mouth, first by mirrored light, next by whispers, and last by vocalized panic, that riders had detached from the army bivouac on the plain and were fast approaching the gorge. At first nobody noticed that throngs of soldiers had begun to appear atop the ravine walls, but Renald certainly did as he heeled Stardust into a gallop down the stream bed.

At the edge of camp, Talking Moon's most trusted braves, complemented by the Penateka, had formed a half-circle around Carne Muerto and the Kiowa and Cheyenne chiefs. Behind, hundreds of their men crowded at the ready. After nosing Stardust to the front, Renald slid from the saddle. From around the jackknife bend came echoing hoof falls, at first very distant. It was minutes until Red Bear and Talking Moon arrived. The erstwhile war chief, unable to gain his mount with his arm slung, had insisted on walking rather than being dragged there in a travois. By then the hoof rumbling had swelled to a thunderous level. Taking his place at the center of the group in his war bonnet, as if still in command, Talking Moon rested himself on a flat stone with a view straight down the gorge to where the stream cut dramatically out of sight. He glowered like a child.

On top of everything else, Renald figured, he was probably suffering a painful hangover. Renald remembered the days when he'd roped a few himself.

Soon two riders rounded the bend. One was uniformed and carried the swallow-tailed regimental colors; the other was in civilian clothes and held a flag of parley. Curious as to who Davidson had sent into the ravine, Renald stepped forward, lifting his spyglasses. Hardly surprised, he grinned at the sight of Sergeant Chance and Cole Hawker flashing looks left and right in the spray their mounts were kicking up. Finally, the pair halted their dripping beasts feet away.

Sergeant Chance traded salutes with Renald before the two men alighted from their mounts, leaving the flag staffs swaying in their deep guidon sockets. Back of Renald, Talking Moon lifted himself with wincing effort to join his fellow chiefs. A hush ensued during which each side evaluated the other, head to foot. The Indians weren't so respectful of the formidable horsemen—one white, the other black— that they didn't look them in the eye. Hawk and Chance extended their attention to the crush of painted warriors behind the chiefs, to the village beyond, and up the high ravine walls to the rows of soldiers presently crenellating the ridgelines. Almost in unison, the white men lowered their eyes.

"This here's Dead Meat," Hawk told Chance. "And that oughta be Chief Red Bear. Respects to you both." He pointed at Talking Moon. "I don't have to ask who Pretty Feathers is."

"No," said Renald. "You don't."

"Just look at them eyes. So he's the nephew, eh? What happened to *him*?"

"She shot him."

Hawk raised his bushy eyebrows. "Oops! She done it again."

Renald was grim. As far as the law was concerned the second bullet didn't count, but she would have to answer for the first one. He found himself suspicious of Hawker's presence, surmising it was opportunistic. "Got yourself a new job?"

Hawk came close. "Whatd'ya mean?"

Renald whispered, "You know what I mean. Who's better qualified to round up and slaughter their horses?"

"Somebody's gotta do it," Hawk whispered. "Is there a lot of 'em? I get paid by the head."

He nodded. "Too many to risk spooking. Comanche know it as well."

Hawk licked his lips. Then, "And the woman? What sorta shape is *she* in? I mean besides the obvious."

"She's all right, thanks to Carne Muerto's Henrys."

"Shifted the balance of power, done they? And what about the boy?"

Renald sighed. "He's being pulled every which way."

"Won't be easy fer him," said Hawk. "Nice kid?"

"Real nice."

"They sure spoil 'em with love, don't they? Fathers stick close to their boys."

In Hawk, Renald saw a softer man than he'd ever thought was there. But that impression was fleeting. Next, the big man lumbered over to Talking Moon, hands on hips. "Ain't you the chief boasts bullets bounce off 'im?" Talking Moon evaded his eyes, leading Hawk to chuckle with contempt.

"Whipped by a woman! So much fer that new medicine you been promising!"

The chief dragged his gaze upward and glared back.

Sergeant Chance broke in. "Please, Mr. Hawker. We're supposed to be offering 'em quarter, not goading 'em into a fight."

"Let's get down to business," said Renald. "What's coming if they surrender?"

Chance shrugged. "What else but the comforts of domestication?" He unbuttoned his chest pocket, withdrew an envelope, and handed it to Renald. "The army begins sort-and-escort this day.

"Pretty confident, ain't you?" Reading the document, Renald reported, "That's what it says. Full amnesty and immediate transfer to Indian Territory. But there's more ..." He eyed his nephew. "Commander Davidson offers Chief Talking Moon a travel pass to visit his son *wherever he shall live*. It bears his signature and stamp."

"White man's promise," the chief growled.

"He didn't have to do it. Maybe with a few extra years on you, you'd recognize the father in his actions."

"Davidson's word is good!" offered Chance. "As for Laura Little ..."

"Hereabouts, the woman is called Whispering Wind," Hawk sneered. He then cupped a hand to one ear, as if listening for something.

"As for Laura Little ..." Chance repeated, "I'm charged with her arrest for the murder of Texas Tonk." To the chiefs he explained, "The woman and her son ride out with us or I leave the truce flag here. You could use it in case them bullets don't bounce."

A long moment passed. While the peace chief remained remote, Carne Muerto and Talking Moon studied each other's faces for signs. The imperative of immediate surrender was sinking in. Doubtless nobody wanted to be the first to concede, not even Red Bear.

Carne Muerto turned fully around, craning his neck. The rows of men on each cliff had thickened into black bands underlining the blue sky. On the northern side, dismounted soldiers were crawling over Double Barrel Rock and winding down into the gorge like an army of ants.

Chance raised his voice to the chiefs. "Don't get the wrong idea. This ain't no siege. We ride outta here without them, three thousand men gonna flood this canyon guns a-blazing."

Renald cautioned Chance. "Best if the elders agree on surrender and inform their clans. That takes an intertribal meeting. Otherwise the warriors could splinter off."

Said Carne Muerto, "Even my men could attempt to get away. Without me."

Talking Moon registered the message. "I not stop dog soldiers if they run. Maybe some Kiowa and Comanche run too. Any brave not marry, no children maybe run."

"That's to be expected," Chance responded. "You surrender your women and children, your aged, your horses, and yourselves—and as many fighting men as'll follow you—and I expect that's enough to prevent a full-on engagement."

The Kiowa and Cheyenne elders stepped forward. A round of troubled looks was exchanged among the chiefs. The Comanche remembered Mackenzie's brutal destruction of their village along the North Fork; the Cheyenne, Custer's obliteration of theirs at the Washita; the Kiowa, the appalling Sand Creek Massacre. This is what they had been fighting back against, yet it was just what could be visited upon them minutes from now. For his part, Talking Moon said nothing.

The new but more moderate war chief stepped before Chance. "We need one hour for council," said Carne Muerto.

Other villages had capitulated in less time when faced with overwhelming force.

"On one condition," replied Tops Chance. "You took money and a horse from Mr. Hawker here. Both belong to the United States Army."

Dead Meat huffed resignedly, then dug into the pouch sashed below his waist and called for somebody to bring forward Texas' pinto. She was fully rigged with government-issue tack, a saddle gun lashed to her side. Without fuss, the chief forfeited both money and beast. At this, a collective gasp escaped from the fighting men. In the murmuring to follow, Hawk told Chance, "That horse didn't much like 'im anyhow."

Chance accepted the packet and transferred it to Hawk. "Take this to Black Jack with my recommendation he signal delay."

Causing more strain on his animal than on himself, Hawk regained his mount. He swung around and gathered the pinto's reins. With that, he tipped his hat at Carne Muerto.

"Hold it, Mr. Hawker," said Chance, eyeing Renald. "The C.O. wants to know about those Hermann brothers."

"Talking Moon says they're in Apache land," said Renald. "I'm halfway there already." A thought struck him, and he regarded his nephew. "They, too, got a father wants 'em returned. Wanna help?"

Choking back the reins of his jumpy horse, Cole Hawker smiled through his beard at the look on Talking Moon's face. Then he rode off.

* * *

At the sight he spotted through his spyglasses, and with a thrill in his voice that his words belied, Lieutenant Colonel John Davidson remarked, "Here comes trouble ..."

Saddled abreast of him at the head of the halted troop column, Cole Hawker responded, "Don't I know it!"

To Hawk's right sat Sergeant Emanuel Chance. "*Trouble,* sir?"

Davidson squinted a second time into his lenses. Out of the gorge rode a woman and child on separate mounts, the boy atop the unmistakable Stardust. Leading them respectively on foot were Talking Moon and Scott Renald. Observed Davidson, "One renegade chief to face sheep farming, one errant scout to face inquiry, one reckless civilian to face trial—and one innocent child to face the consequences."

Receiving the glasses from Davidson, Hawk marveled, "Born injun, that boy'll die white."

In turn, he passed the binoculars to Chance.

Sighting the group, the sergeant put in, "There's Scott Renald. He's sure holding his head high."

"High?" Davidson smoothed his whiskers. "Let's see how high he holds that big chin of his at his court-martial."

"Oh, I wager he will, sir!" Chance swelled his uniform with a drag of warm air. "There's a fella rode into the desert lonesome and come back with a family."

"Well," Davidson sighed, spurring his charger ahead, "let's go meet the Renalds ..."

Afterword
or
"Whatever Happened to Randolph Scott?"

There would be no *Comanche Captive* without Randolph Scott's penultimate film, *Comanche Station* (1960), written by Burt Kennedy, directed by Budd Boetticher, and produced by Scott and his longtime collaborator Harry Joe Brown.

The story of a man who fights to return a liberated Indian captive to her family inspired this author to imagine the same situation with a key alteration: the family she's determined to return to is her tribal one.

This book became something of a tribute to Randolph Scott and the dazzling horse he rode through so many adventures. Along with Joel McCrea and John Wayne, Scott is one of the most convincing screen presences ever to ride tall in the saddle; and the saddle he rode in the most belonged to a magnificent flaxen sorrel whose name *offscreen* was Stardust.

It is my hope that Scott fans have found in this text a satisfying reply to The Statler Brothers' nostalgic hit single, "Whatever Happened to Randolph Scott?"

Acknowledgments

The literary influences on *Comanche Captive* range from first-hand accounts of Indian abductions to Louis L'Amour's thrilling, sand-biting *Taggart* (1959), for its depictions of people's struggles amidst and against a rugged terrain. Hollywood Westerns of the post–World War II era had a greater impact, and the text pays them plenty of homage. For every Western novel I've read, I've seen a hundred Western films. Besides the aforementioned *Comanche Station*, movies to which this narrative owes special mention are Robert Mulligan's haunting *The Stalking Moon* and John Ford's irresistibly lovable cavalry pictures, especially the alternately melancholic and lighthearted *She Wore a Yellow Ribbon* (1949).

For help with Comanche words and phrases, I'm grateful to Martin Flores of the Comanche Nation, and Carney Saupitty, Jr. of the Comanche National Museum and Cultural Center. Sadly, I'm told that as few as ten fluent speakers of the Comanche language remain. Mr. Flores' assistance extended to making recordings of himself speaking the language used in the text so I might hear it for myself. From Mr. Saupitty, I was fascinated to learn that the word *taiboo* (white person) is a corruption of *tuboo*, a word for an instrument "one can write with, draw with, or paint with." The Comanche first came to call the white man *tuboo* after exposure to the painter George Catlin and the troops he travelled west with in the early 1800s. They concluded that "the first thing a white man will do is draw you, paint you, or write in their journal about you."

Finally, I wish to thank writer David Speranza, a former colleague of mine at *The Prague Revue,* for his critical early reading of the manuscript, and the fine editorial team at Cengage's Five Star imprint, which published the hardback in 2017.

About the Author

Born in Minneapolis in 1968, D. László Conhaim's first professional writing credit was a two-part 1986 interview in Los Angeles and Tokyo with Japanese film legend Toshiro Mifune for Minnesota weekly *City Pages*. In 1995, Conhaim co-founded *The Prague Revue*, the longest-running literary journal to serve the community of international writers in Prague. For *TPR*, he wrote a fictional remembrance of Miguel de Unamuno, "Feeling into Don Miguel," which Gore Vidal "read with delight" and Alexander Zaitchik (*Rolling Stone, The Nation*) called "masterful" in *Think Magazine*. In 1999, TPR Books published his corresponding novel *Autumn Serenade*. In 2017, Cengage/Five Star released *Comanche Captive* in hardback, the first installment of a Western trilogy whose direct sequel is slated for release in late 2021. In 2019, the trilogy's chronological conclusion, *All Man's Land* (Broken Arrow Press), was published to acclaim. The story of an ex-slave who seeks justice from the lawman who once owned him, *All Man's Land* was selected Finalist Best Traditional Western Novel, 2020 Western Writers of America Spur Awards. Conhaim lives in Israel.

CPSIA information can be obtained
at www.ICGtesting.com
Printed in the USA
LVHW111512100820
662829LV00003B/896